Dragon Foretold

Dragon Point #4

Eve Langlais

New York Times Bestselling Author

Copyright © September 2016, Eve Langlais
Cover Art by Yocla Designs © August 2016
Edited by Devin Govaere
2nd Edit by Amanda Pederick
Copy Edited by Literally Addicted to Detail
Line Edits by Brieanna Robertson
Produced in Canada

Published by Eve Langlais
1606 Main Street, PO Box 151
Stittsville, Ontario, Canada, K2S1A3
http://www.EveLanglais.com

ISBN: 978 1988 328 56 0

Chapter One

Many years ago, when all was right in the world and shifters hid under cloaks of humanity, there was a young, impressionable girl named Sue-Ellen Mercer.

It's so grand.

Uncle's house awed simple Sue-Ellen. Just look at it with its huge windows. She'd wager they were the quality kind that didn't fog at temperature changes and could open with a slight push that didn't require a stick to keep it propped.

What of the front entrance? Comprised of two doors, the wood carved and smooth, tall enough for giants! Surely only the rich and fabulous ever stepped through them.

The lawn looked softer than any rug Sue-Ellen ever recalled gracing their house. Huge and manicured, the grass was just like a living, plush, green carpet.

All in all, everything appeared absolutely stunning. She'd never seen such a beautiful home. Never imagined this kind of wealth. And if her family had their way, she'd have never experienced it.

Why do they shun this rich extension of our family?

Against her mother's wishes, Sue-Ellen had come for a visit with her uncle Theo and her aunt

Hattie—who looked nothing like her tired and worn sister. How could Sue-Ellen say no when the car with the lovely new interior arrived? It had all the bells and whistles, including climate control and air-conditioned seats. Who cooled their butt in a car?

Rich folks did.

The new sedan with its gleaming black paint and soft leather seats—buttery soft and oh so decadent—sure beat the rusty old pickup the Mercer family used to get around.

Uncle Theo himself seemed the height of suave sophistication, dressed in a business suit with a tie. The only time any of her brothers wore a tie was when someone died. And then, after a few toasts with alcohol—fermented for at least a few full moons—they would wrap them around their heads bandana style and wrestle because, according to her ma, that was what men did instead of dealing with their feelings.

Uncle Theo wasn't like that. Uncle Theo was always properly dressed. Always the height of elegance, with the most impressive manners she'd ever heard. It made a young girl wonder what kind of lifestyle her mysterious uncle led.

Despite him being married to her sister, Sue-Ellen's mother didn't like or respect the man. Even when Hattie asked—and so nicely too with that soft southern accent—Sue-Ellen's ma had vehemently argued against Hattie and Theo taking any of the kids for a visit.

Sue-Ellen's mother appeared determined to keep all of her children in the shack they called home. Much too full of pride—which didn't pay the bills—Ma didn't want them accepting gifts or a helping hand. "We don't need no charity. We do fine on our own."

Did they? Was doing fine wearing hand-me-downs that were already hand-me-downs? Eating expired food because it was bought at a fraction of the cost? And her mother could have totally been on that coupon show, given she hoarded the best ones and then used them to devastating effect. Grocery stores cringed when they saw her coming armed with children, grocery carts, and her binder.

Sue-Ellen wasn't completely ignorant. She knew why her mother did it. Not having a man around and too many mouths to feed meant Ma had to do what she could to make ends meet.

I understand that. She respected it, too, but it didn't stop Sue-Ellen from wanting the better things in life. She wanted to know what the world looked like when not living below the poverty threshold. She didn't see the problem with accepting her aunt's and uncle's offer to visit. Sure, Ma hated Uncle Theo, but he was family, and how could her ma be so cruel, given how fragile Auntie's health was? Even more tenuous since her children had fled the nest, leaving Auntie alone.

The arguments with her mother only bolstered Sue-Ellen's resolve so that, when her uncle left, he had an extra passenger stowed in the back.

When discovered, he didn't threaten to take her back home or tell her she'd done wrong. He'd looked at her and smiled. "I'm glad you decided to join me and your aunt, niece."

So was she. Eating at a sit-down restaurant for lunch later that day with real tablecloths and a menu on actual paper, Sue-Ellen didn't regret her choice—even if the phone call with her mother turned out quite shrill.

But she'd heard Ma screaming her entire life. It was hard to feel bad, seeing as how Auntie and Uncle had done nothing but spoil Sue-Ellen since her arrival. Showering her with clothes and gifts, her every wish catered to. Treated just like their daughter.

Here, she got all the attention and didn't have to share with rowdy brothers. Here, she never lacked for food—and didn't have to lick it to claim it. She wore the best clothes—new clothes and not off a discount rack. She had an aunt who smelled almost like her mother. A woman who had time to brush her hair and tell her how pretty she was.

It wasn't that her own mother didn't care, but Ma was busy. Once their father died, she had to work twice as hard, especially given that Sue-Ellen had a few brothers always breaking stuff and getting into trouble. Some houses had swear jars with money; theirs had one with bail funds.

It wasn't a life for a young lady. In her mind, her mother was better off with one less mouth to feed—or so she'd convinced herself.

Sue-Ellen, having tasted the good life, never wanted to return to the swamp and the crowded shack they called home. She liked having her own room with clean linens and her own bathroom. There were nice things in her drawers. And the food? Not freshly caught from the bayou every evening.

So if she loved living here so much, why did she jeopardize it all by sneaking into Uncle's office in the middle of the night?

What am I doing?

Showing her roots, obviously. Grandpa always said they were descended from thieves. Smugglers, too, which meant stealing into her uncle's office happened with confident ease. Stealth was in her blood.

Sue-Ellen had no problem getting to the main floor, and the door to Uncle's office gave at a simple turn of the knob. She eased inside and slowly shut the slab of thick wood behind her.

Click.

Breath held, she froze. Had anyone heard? Would someone demand to know what she was doing?

What's my excuse?

The dark side of her didn't think she needed one, especially if she ate any witnesses.

No need to get primal. Nothing happened.

Sue-Ellen let loose a breath and realized that she was shaking—with adrenaline, not fear. Being good all the time was hard. Sneaking around and checking out stuff had an element of danger, which in turn, energized her. It felt great, but the real reason she did all this was because her curiosity required satisfaction.

Earlier that day, Uncle obviously hadn't known she was outside his office in the bushes, looking for the mini drone she'd managed to crash again. Just one of the many toys they'd bought to amuse their teen niece.

Peeking through the window, Sue-Ellen saw her uncle doing something mysterious. It wasn't just cats that suffered from an inquisitive nature.

Now, here in his office, past the witching hour, she tried to recreate her uncle's actions. It took fiddling with a few books on the shelf before she tilted the right one.

Tick.

With hardly a whisper of sound, the section of the bookcase in front of her pulled into the wall then slid sideways.

Holy shit.

Her mother wasn't there to screech, "Potty mouth!"

Then again, her ma might have said something even more inappropriate, given the moving bookcase revealed a door-sized opening with stairs going down. Talk about Scooby-Doo cool. A secret basement. What did Uncle hide down there?

Perhaps he'd built himself a place to go when the full moon begged for him to swap skins. Those with a wolf as their animal tended to be very driven by the phases of the moon. Sue-Ellen, being of the alligator variety, was drawn to raw chicken and squishy mud.

She missed rolling in the muck and then sluicing off in the swamp. She'd not been able to change since her arrival.

A place to be myself would be nice.

For a girl who'd grown up on the edge of

the bayou and could slip into her gator skin for a swim anytime she liked, the lack of privacy to be herself was the one jarring negative note in paradise.

I miss being me. Even if her version of *me* would terrify most people and send them running for a shotgun. Gator skin made for nice purses. Although her grandmother always swore snake was better.

Sue-Ellen skipped down the steps, her slipper socks silent on the metal stairs. It was a narrow descent, and a strange, almost antiseptic smell permeated the air. Whatever hid below, Uncle kept it clean.

Was this Uncle's secret lair? Or did he keep treasure down here? Everyone in the family knew Uncle Theo and Auntie Hattie were rich. The kind of rich she'd only seen on television until now.

So why am I jeopardizing it? Why did she sneak around? Nothing good ever came from subterfuge. It was how her great-uncle had gotten shot. "Served him right for visiting that Jezebel" was the general consensus among the women in the family.

The stairs ended, and she entered into a storage room, a decently-sized space with racks of wooden shelves set in rows on either side as she stepped off the final tread. Bottles of wine sat cradled on the many levels, and she could have groaned in disappointment.

A wine cellar. Nothing more than a hidden stash of vintage bottles. What a letdown.

She turned around, ready to head back up, when she noted a line of white along the floor at the end of one aisle.

The slash of light drew her, and she ghosted down the slim path, ignoring the corked bottles—pretending she wasn't afraid they'd suddenly pop and hit her like little wooden bullets.

Nothing exploded, and she made it to the wall, a wall showing a thin streak of light where the floor met it.

It could mean only one thing.

A hidden room.

Her excitement level spiked. Forget about going back to bed. She had a new mystery to solve. *Just call me Daphne.* With dirty-blonde hair and jeans.

Sue-Ellen felt around for a lever, something to give her access. A hook on the wall pulled down, and the door clicked open.

Inside, another room, with more shelving, the metal kind this time, holding boxes, some of them still wrapped in plastic. Boring.

But do you know what wasn't boring? The stack of boxes on a skid at the far side that moved with a simple shove and revealed a door with a keypad.

Another room. A locked one. Be still her beating heart.

The problem with curiosity? Once ignited, it wouldn't go away; it only got stronger. Sue-Ellen couldn't resist. What was in the room beyond the door?

Despite knowing full well how stupid she was being, Sue-Ellen couldn't fight the allure. *I have to know.*

She pressed her ear against the door. Listened. Heard nothing. Not a damned thing.

As for her inner self? That cold predator who had a special sense for danger? It remained quiet.

Her hand wrapped around the handle and gripped it, but it didn't even turn a little. She peered at the keypad. Interestingly enough, it looked just like the one upstairs by the front door. Would it respond to the same codes?

Quickly, she tapped in her uncle's nine digits. She hadn't purposely memorized them when her uncle used the system. Remembering stuff was just the kind of thing that came naturally to her—and was probably inherited from her great-grandpa, a renowned bank robber who did so love cracking safes.

The series of digits worked. The door clicked, and the handle turned. She took a deep breath before she opened it. Well greased, the hinges made not a sound. Then again, it might not have been heard, given the hum emanating from the room.

Initially, Sue-Ellen blinked at what she saw. It took a moment to process because what she encountered wasn't what she'd expected.

She'd thought maybe she'd find some kind of drug den or a secret sex place for kinky stuff. She watched television. She read. She knew what adults did in hiding.

First thing she noted, however, was a counter to the left of the door, stainless steel and empty, set over gunmetal-gray cabinets. No beakers or burners adorned the surface to make drugs. Nor did she see signs of winemaking equipment.

Pushing the door wider, she noted the counter extended the length of the wall in what turned out to be a huge room. Farther in, the metal surface held things—machines with blinking lights, glass vials snug in plastic stands, microscopes. At the far end, there was a fridge, a tall metal thing of industrial size that made her wonder what it held inside. Bodies perhaps? More and more intriguing.

Her gaze kept tracking the large room, unable to take it all in with a single glance. A sharp breath sucked in when she noted a bed in the middle of the room. The kind of bed usually seen only in hospitals, with metal rails and wheels.

It was occupied.

The back portion of it was raised, placing the guy on it in a sitting position. His eyes were closed.

A sheet drawn to mid-chest hid most of him from sight, except for his left arm. That arm lay strapped to a metal ledge projecting from the railing of the bed. They had it exposed because of the IV.

The tube trailing from his arm was filled with some dark fluid. The line of plastic traveled to a bag that grew plumper as she watched. It filled with his blood.

Sue-Ellen took a step closer, noting his fine features. A boy, not much older than she. He wore a hospital gown, the kind that tied in the back, except his appeared loose as it listed off a shoulder.

Closer. She couldn't help but be drawn to this boy hidden under her uncle's house.

Who was he? Not a cousin for sure, she knew all of them by face and name. Sue-Ellen didn't see any family resemblance in the boy at all.

Good thing because Ma said it's a sin to love one's cousin. It was why they didn't talk to cousins Patty and Thelma anymore.

This guy had features that looked as if they were chiseled from stone. Greek stone, given his square jaw and straight nose. His short hair was a dark blond at the roots and lightened at the tips. She wondered if it would shimmer in the sun if allowed to grow long. One thing for sure, he was incredibly handsome.

"Who are you?" she whispered.

Oddest thing, she could have sworn she heard a whisper. "*Mine.*"

Chapter Two

Who am I? Sometimes, he didn't remember. Didn't know. Didn't care.

In the sea of nothingness in which he floated, he heard a voice. A feminine voice. The notes of it soft and lilting. An angel's voice surely.

Had he finally died and gone to heaven?

That would irritate the scientists playing with him. He was their golden child. The one they were banking on for their research. Because of them, his life was a never-ending battery of tests. And more tests.

They just couldn't get enough of him. Poking and prodding, siphoning all the fluids they dared. Surely, he'd run out of blood one day. It hadn't happened yet. His steady diet of red meat and leafy salads, apparently the perfect balance, made sure his veins were always plump.

"Can you even hear me?"

The soft voice teased at him from beyond the barrier of sleep. The doctors often made him sleep now, citing his difficulty in being managed.

I don't want to be managed.

Obedience was overrated in his opinion, and he didn't believe in being shy when it came to voicing his thoughts.

"Fuck you. I don't have to do what you say." Brave words, but no match when pitted against four guards—full-grown men meant to restrain him for his own good.

A boy could only do so much.

Rebellion got him nowhere, and his acts of defiance meant they kept him drugged. He slept most of the time now, and the moments where waking was allowed, his muscles, his entire being, moved sluggishly.

For now, at least. A smart boy—just ask the many tests that said so—he didn't let the doctors know the drugs had less and less effect. His body was learning how to fight off the narcotics. And once he shed them for good?

I won't be their lab rat anymore.

"Can you hear me?"

Yes. His finger twitched, which really wasn't what he'd planned to do. He'd meant to lift his head, open his eyes, and talk.

He'd failed miserably.

"Your poor thing. Are you sick? Is that why Uncle keeps you hidden?"

Not sick.

"Are you my cousin?"

I hope not. The angel visiting him had a nice voice. A voice he could listen to all day.

"I wish you could tell me why they're draining your blood."

Because they need it for their nefarious plans. Cue an evil laugh.

"I wish you could talk and tell me what's going on." Her voice sounded so close now. Her demand so simple.

He could do this. He could lift his head.

Nope.

Talk.

His lips didn't move.

But his eyes did flutter, and the blurry world outside sharpened.

Brown eyes met his. Eyes that glowed with inhuman intensity.

It didn't freak him out. *Because mine glow, too.*

And the beast in him, the one that wanted to rampage forth, stirred. It whispered. A sibilant hiss of sound, *Isss mine.*

Mine.

The word echoed again, ringing within him with the force of a bell. And his lips moved, whispering it aloud. "Mine."

Unfortunately, she misunderstood his claim.

Chapter Three

"What's yours?" Sue-Ellen wondered what the boy on the bed meant. It was hard to think when the most beautiful eyes she'd ever seen stared at her. Gold irises that glowed.

What is he?

"Hey, you!"

The shout startled her, and she looked over her shoulder to see that a man in a white coat had appeared via another door. His expression appeared quite stern, and the spectacles on his nose magnified his gaze. He was also one hundred percent human, while the boy in the bed—she inhaled another breath—resembled nothing and no one she'd ever encountered.

"What are you doing to him?" she asked.

"None of your business. You're not supposed to be here," the fellow in the white coat exclaimed.

"Indeed, she's not. It would seem someone has rudely taken advantage of my hospitality." The voice of her uncle, coming from behind, startled. Especially given its cold tone.

Whirling, Sue-Ellen saw her uncle Theo dressed in a thick plaid-patterned robe. Tousled hair meant he'd come from his bed, and his lips were turned down in displeasure.

Guilt filled her. She knew she shouldn't have come down here. He had a right to his anger, but…

A golden gaze bolstered her. She pointed to the boy. "Why is he here? What are you doing to him?"

"None of your business."

"You're holding him prisoner."

"Am I?"

"He's tied down."

"For his own good."

"I don't believe you." Because something about this seemed so wrong.

"Are you accusing me of something, niece?"

"You're taking his blood."

"Have you never heard of a transfusion?" Her uncle arched a brow.

"Transfusions go two ways."

"Are you a doctor now? And here I thought you still in high school."

Only a year away from graduating, actually, thank you very much. "Why do you have him hidden in your basement?"

"Hardly hidden since you found him. And now you need to unfind this place. Go back to your room."

She didn't move. "Not until I know you're not doing anything wrong."

At that, his brow furrowed, and the expression on his face gave her a chill. "You dare to question me, niece?"

Yes, she did, because there was something very vulnerable about the boy on the bed. Like her, he was young, his skin unmarked by time; he didn't even have any stubble. She noted the rugged line of his jaw, the sculpted line of his lips. He lay in bed, and yet she could tell he was tall but slight of frame. A boy still transitioning to manhood. If she had to guess, she was probably a touch younger.

He was also tied down. A prisoner.

She turned back to him, noting his eyes were closed again. Had she imagined their brief golden glow?

"Move away from the boy."

"Why? Is he contagious?" Because she seemed hotter than before, almost as if a fever took her.

Ignoring her uncle, Sue-Ellen moved closer to the boy. Close enough that she could reach out and touch—if she dared.

"Are you awake?" she asked.

Instead of a reply, his head lifted. It took a brief flutter of lashes before his eyes opened. At first, they appeared dark amber. A spark lit within them, interest and something else. Something that made her tummy flip.

"Hi there," she said. What else did one say to a boy waking in such odd circumstances?

She could have sworn she heard a whispered, *"Hello."*

"Can you hear me?" she asked, cocking her head to the side.

"Can you?"

Again, those words, oddly spoken, as if directly to her mind.

The eyes still staring at her blazed brighter.

Bright as the sun. Who didn't want to touch the sun?

She reached out, fingers stretching toward his face, only to pause. *What if he is contagious?*

His nostrils flared. *I am not sick.*

Perhaps not. Still…

"Move away." Uncle's demand, instead, caused her to drop her hand and press it against the boy's.

Sparks ignited. Seriously, it felt as if the point of contact had received a huge jolt.

Her lips parted as golden fire ignited in his gaze. She'd never seen such a thing. "What are you?" She breathed the question.

"None of your business, so take your hand off him," snapped her uncle. "Hurry up with the needle, Vernon."

What needle?

Something pinched her arm. She whirled to see the man in the white coat withdrawing a syringe.

Her eyes widened. "What did you inject me with?"

She wavered on her feet and turned a panicked gaze to the boy on the bed. She reached out. "Help me."

He yelled, "No!" and surged forth.

But his restraints bound him. As the sheets fell from his chest, the straps were revealed, winding around his torso, tethering his arms, and his legs she'd wager, too, even as her thoughts slowed.

She blinked and wondered what had happened to her because she could swear his skin bulged. Rippled as if something under it looked to escape.

The fight with her knees ended, and she hit the floor. Muffled, as if from a distance, she heard the murmur of voices, but she could make no sense of the words.

"Look at him…"

"He's changing."

Why did they sound so surprised? She wished she could understand, but her mind moved sluggishly. Her eyelashes fluttered, her lids so heavy and…

I think I need a nap.

Chapter Four

She collapsed.

He didn't know who the girl was. Didn't know much more than she had the most amazing eyes. The softest looking lips. The sweetest scent.

She was a stranger, and yet, he didn't like it one bit when she fell.

Muscles bulged and strained, pushing against his straps. They held. He couldn't escape to save her, so he turned an evil stare on the doctor still holding the guilty syringe.

"You killed her." The words emerged low and growly.

Theodore Parker, the man who'd recently come into his life, courtesy of his guardian Anastasia, slapped Dr. Michaels on the back. He wore his habitual smirk. "Vernon didn't kill the girl. I don't want her dead. She is, after all, family. She's merely sleeping. Deeply. But she won't suffer any lasting effects because, you never know, she might be useful later."

"You can't use her." He uttered the words with the utmost dark and deadly sincerity.

Parker arched a brow. "Really? Why not?"

Because she's mine. He almost said the damning words out loud. "Do whatever you like to the girl. I don't care." Such a lie. He did give a damn. He just couldn't do anything about it.

"So you mean to say you wouldn't care if I hurt her?"

He didn't say a word, but his nostrils flared. Parker noticed. The man watched and analyzed everything.

The sadistic bastard bent over and rose a moment later, his fist knotted in the girl's hair, lifting her by it. A good thing she remained unconscious. It would hurt.

He daresss to hurt her.

He couldn't restrain a roar and, once again, strained at his bonds. He snarled. Snapped. His body rippled again, something under his skin desperate to get out.

Ssset me free.

"Excellent," Parker crooned with the most villainous of glee. "Keep going, boy. Keep changing."

"I won't." He took deep breaths. Tried to calm his racing heart. Ignored the thing inside him that whispered, the sibilance of it frightening and cold.

Also very alluring.

"You will change. It's past time you did. Why do you persist in fighting it?" Parker angled the girl's head so he appeared to speak to her. "You never fought your lizard inside"—Parker turned his head once more—"I remember her mother bragging to my wife about how early she learned to shift. The girl has the most excellent genes. Not as good as yours, of course"—Parker shot him a sneer—"but excellent for so many purposes."

"Leave her alone."

"Or what? You can't do anything as you are right now. You can't stop me."

Yesss, I can. The dark voice inside flowed through him, and for a moment, just a moment, their thoughts became one.

The incredible raw beauty—and the darkness of it—almost won.

No. He couldn't let it take over. He had to stop. He shouldn't do it. Shouldn't give Parker what he wanted.

But the thing inside him, the thing dormant up until now, wanted out.

Ssset me free.

It shoved at his skin. Expanded it in ways that skin surely should not be stretched. He tamped it down.

"I guess I was mistaken. You don't care about the girl." Parker shook her. A sly expression entered Parker's gaze. "Maybe I should see if someone else wants her."

Once again, he couldn't control himself. He arched against the straps, straining with all his might, but he didn't have the muscle to break free.

Not in this form. But he was more than just this compact body.

Let me out, the voice whispered. It knocked at his mind's walls. It begged to come in.

If he did, if he let whatever beast nestled inside him escape, he would give Parker what he wanted.

Embrace your true self.

If he did, if he allowed the chill consciousness to take over, would he still be him?

If you don't accept, you'll be a prisoner forever.

Truth or lie? Did it matter?

Things couldn't get worse.

Parker yanked the girl higher, the strain on her hair surely excruciating. Good thing she slept, but he didn't like it. *You don't hurt what's mine.*

"Release the girl."

"Who, this girl? You don't get to tell me what to do with her. I'm her uncle. I decide." Parker pivoted and faced a mirror, a two-way glass that recorded everything. "Anyone watching want the girl since he doesn't?"

How dare Parker offer the girl? "Is your honor so lacking you'd offer your niece to just anyone?"

"Honor doesn't give you money and power." Parker tossed a smile over his shoulder, the lupine in him showing with the gleam of teeth. "Some pieces, like my niece, are expendable. I can always borrow another. The Mercers tend to procreate like rabbits."

I will chew his face.

Raw. The idea didn't come from him, but the rumble of tummy was real.

"Come on, surely there is someone who wants her?"

It was Dr. Michaels, the bastard who liked to hurt him, who said, "I'll take her."

Over his dead body.

Crush him into a pulp.

He'd love to. But first, he'd need a little help.

Help me do this.

Just close your eyes and let me in.

It proved easy to do, like opening a mental door and inviting in a friend. A friend who swirled around him and squeezed like a close hug.

Soon, he couldn't recall why he'd hesitated. Why had he not agreed to this before?

He felt so strong. And squished.

This body, this entire shape, was much too small and compact.

I should be light and airy. Fix it.

It took a big heave. A bit of straining. The skin initially resisted, but finally it turned, changed to scales he saw as he opened his eyes. Finely shaped and dull.

It also hurt.

He roared at the pain.

Roared? He shouldn't have that kind of pitch and sound, and yet he did, and even as the pain washed through him again, his body crackling and moving, the tenor changed once more.

He bucked at the tight straps binding him. His body fought against them as it thickened. Metal popped as the buckle exploded from the pressure. Next to go, the gown, which shredded and fell from him.

He sprang from the bed, feeling bigger and stronger. But not yet complete.

This was not his final form. Something moved at his back.

Wings. Knobby things still trying to unfurl.

Massively unwieldy things, just like this body was wrong. All wrong.

He became bigger still, his skin pushing and pulling, the scales popping off and revealing a new layer of armor. His true skin.

With a final euphorically painful rush, he exploded into something massive, and yet so light.

And bright.

Blazing gold filled the room, and the wings at his back fluttered. He flexed his claws and reveled in his power. So much power.

Because I am dragon!

The creature before him studied him with awe and yet didn't bow.

Silly puppy. I am better than you.

He glared down at the offending creature, and yet the man didn't cower as he should. Instead, he held something in front of him. A smaller creature with strange, wheat-colored hair.

Food? He sniffed and noted the scent belonged to him.

Mine.

He reached out to grab but halted as the male holding her took on some wolfish traits. His face projected into a skin-covered muzzle, and his fingers grew wicked claws. Claws that rested across her throat.

"Don't move."

The words were understood. The man and beast had merged. They knew everything.

And this man before him, this Parker, he would regret his actions. Did this little wolf not understand who was truly the power here?

In that instant, he grasped something extremely important. Something he'd never realized before.

No wonder the doctors had kept him drugged. No wonder they wanted a piece of him. Who wouldn't? After all, the universe revolved around him.

I am greater than you. Grander than everyone.

He laughed, and yet the sound emerged as a trill. He took a step forward, and the wolf called Parker drew a claw over the female's throat. Beads of blood appeared. "Don't move another muscle, or I'll kill her. I have a feeling you don't want that."

No. He didn't. For some reason, this girl, this fragile creature he'd just met, meant something to him.

Mine. My angel. He stood still.

Parker smirked. "Wise move. Now, listen up, boy, because this is what's going to happen."

He agreed to too many things that day. Things to save one girl. A stranger. Someone he might never see again but that Parker promised would not come to harm.

It seemed even captives could suffer from chivalry.

And whenever he wondered—usually in violent fashion—if he'd made the right choice, wondered if it were worth the many hours spent alone in the dark, Parker would bring her.

There would be no warning. One moment, he'd be tearing at his restraints, refusing to behave, and then she'd appear. Her face ashen the moment she beheld him.

His angel always cried, fat tears rolling down her cheeks as she held out her hand.

Idiot that he was, he used to grab it back, holding on to her fingers a moment too long, feeling that same jolt every time. Knowing she felt it, too, which made her sob only harder. She would whisper over and over, "I'm sorry. So sorry."

Sorry for what? The fact that Parker was a brilliant lunatic who knew what to use against him?

Even a dragon of his stature had to respect the fact that Parker had found his weakness.

I wonder how much respect he'll have for me when I tear his head from his shoulders and drink from him. That day would come.

Despite what Parker thought, the captivity didn't weaken him. His hatred only grew. But through it all, one thing never changed.

He never stopped protecting her.

Chapter Five

I can't believe it's been almost six years. Six years of living as a prisoner and yet appearing to the world as a rich debutante. Such a lucky girl. After all, not all nieces got plucked from poverty and adopted as daughters.

How Sue-Ellen wished she could go back in time and turn back the clocks. Never hide in her uncle's car.

But if she'd done that, then she would have never met him. The man who would control the rest of her life.

And she didn't mean her uncle.

The first time she met Samael—because yes, the boy in the bed had a name—she'd woken to find herself in her bed, dressed in her nightclothes as if she'd never gone exploring. She remembered what happened next vividly…

Ma didn't raise no fool. Sue-Ellen had immediately marched to her uncle's office to yank on the books, only nothing she did triggered the secret doorway.

Auntie heard Sue-Ellen's ranting—the words quite epic in their colorful and vulgar nature. She wrung her hands, exclaiming, "Is she on drugs, Theo? I won't have her doing drugs in my house."

Auntie was the one who liked to pop a little something or other in the evenings, "to calm her nerves," she claimed. More like catch butterflies and slur her words, especially when chased with a glass of wine—or four.

"Open this up," Sue-Ellen demanded.

"Open what, dear niece?" Uncle Theo replied.

"The door. The one that goes to your secret lab in the basement."

"I don't know what you're talking about." Said with utmost conviction.

He could have been a Mercer he lied so well. "Don't bullshit me."

"Language," Aunt Hattie gasped.

"He knows what I'm talking about. That place I saw last night. Don't deny it. You were there. You drugged me to get me away from that boy."

"None of that happened." Uncle Theo shook his head. "I was in bed all night with Hattie. I think perhaps you might have had a vivid dream. Perhaps the mushrooms at dinner were to blame. A bad one in the mix. I'll speak to our cook."

But she knew it wasn't a dream or magic 'shrooms. Nothing that vivid and emotionally wrenching could be a fabrication. Besides, she had that cold inner voice of her gator telling her something had happened.

That boy is still down there somewhere. I have to find him.

Rescuing him was part of the reason she hadn't left that same day and run back to the bayou.

Not that she could leave. Uncle made it clear Sue-Ellen couldn't go anywhere.

She could still hear him claim he kept her, "Because I promised your brothers I'd take care of you." More like he used her as a bargaining tool to keep them in line. Them and a certain boy.

Weeks after that first nocturnal adventure, right around graduation time, Uncle had commanded her presence in his office. She recalled every moment of that incident, as well.

She'd expected a gift. It was what the other kids at her rich prep school got. For hitting the honor roll, Sue-Ellen got a brand-new car, but that wasn't the reason for her requested presence.

Uncle Theo had other plans for her. When he slid the bookcase aside, the control hidden on his phone, she screeched, "Liar! I knew that was there."

"If you want to live long enough to graduate college, then you'll pretend you don't," Uncle Theo warned.

Sue-Ellen didn't doubt he'd kill her. Uncle Theo, she'd learned, wasn't one to let laws and common decency get in his way.

"I want to see him," she demanded.

"Be my guest." Uncle Theo swept a hand, and she skipped down the stairs.

It took but a second to notice the place had changed since her last visit. The seam of light along the wall was gone. The hook when pulled revealed a touch pad that required her uncle's palm print. The scanner for the next door took a retina scan.

Someone had tightened security. But Sue-

Ellen wouldn't let that stop her from saving the boy.

I'll find a way.

The room with all the medical equipment hadn't changed much, but the bed had turned into a cage. And in that cage, paced the boy.

He whirled at hearing them enter and snarled at Parker, only to gasp a moment later. "Angel."

She ran to him, only stopping at his sharply barked, "Don't touch the bars; they're electrified."

She had to content herself with staring, noting he was much too gaunt and still so very handsome.

"How can I help you?" she whispered, tears rolling down her cheeks. It hurt her to see him in the cage.

"You're safe? No one has harmed you?"

What an odd question. He was the one in a cage.

"The girl hasn't come to harm. And now that you've seen her, you'll do what Dr. Michaels says."

The boy's lips pulled into a tight line, but he nodded.

What did Parker mean? What did the doctor want from him?

She reached out to touch him, careful of the bars, and their fingertips met, a brief touch that jolted her with awareness.

And then she was taken away.

But she saw him again. Every few weeks or so. Never more than a few weeks, a month or so apart. She began to understand that Uncle Theo used Sue-Ellen as a reward for good behavior.

And in time, that had paid off. The boy became a man, and less than two years after their first meeting, Parker let him out of his cage.

The boy was no longer a prisoner. The boy also had a name—Samael.

Nowadays, instead of being subjected to a battery of tests, Samael lived in plain sight. He attended the best college and went into the strangest field. Archeology.

Parker was quite excited by it. Sue-Ellen wasn't crazy about all the girls that flocked to him, fawning over his blond hair, good looks, and easy smile.

"You're like a hot and young version of Professor Jones," she grumbled during one of their stolen moments. Those kisses were exchanged in hiding, hot and heavy. The zap of recognition they'd shared as they managed fleeting touches while he'd been held prisoner had long ago stopped, but the pitter-patter of her heart still happened whenever he was in the room.

That pitter-patter was why she'd never left her uncle's care. She didn't give a whit about her uncle's threats. If Sue-Ellen had wanted to leave, she could have. It would have been so simple.

Her brother, Brandon, had tried to rescue her at one point, and it just about broke her heart to send him away. But it was for the best. She couldn't leave her dear uncle until she could help Samael escape.

Although, more and more, she wondered if

he wanted to get away. Samael certainly didn't act like a man bound. As a matter of fact, just recently, he had been allowed to travel halfway across the world on some kind of archeological dig.

Samael claimed he stuck around to keep her safe. But she had to wonder because, more and more, she noted him giving the orders—and others jumping to obey.

Did that have to do with the fact that Samael was the heir to a long-lost throne? She knew he was a very special kind of dragon.

He's an imposter.

The voice came to her as usual without notice. She'd begun to think of it as her conscience. A conscience that sounded an awful lot like the old Samael.

Don't tell me I preferred it when he was an unwilling patient?

How awful of her. And yet, at times, she really missed the other him.

He, on the other hand, didn't seem to miss her as much. She'd barely seen him since he'd struck it famous on that dig he'd taken over when that professor went missing.

The excavation Samael had headed was considered the find of the century. Historians were calling it a treasure unlike any they'd seen.

Rumor had it Samael had found a dragon hoard. Because, guess what, dragons did exist.

And Samael was one of them.

Chapter Six

"This is bullshit," Samael reiterated as he adjusted his cuffs. The fine linen shirt he wore was tailored to his shape, and the gold cufflinks added that extra touch of elegance.

"Watch your language. You are a man of distinction now," Anastasia lectured. She was always lecturing him on his manners.

Nag.

"Don't tell me what to do." Samael had learned a while ago who truly held the power in their dynamic. *Without me, she is nothing.* "Don't forget who you're talking to."

"And you seem to forget who I am."

"The high priestess of the Golden religion. Blah. Blah. Blah. I know. I've heard about it my entire life. But guess what, I am the reason you even have a religion, so you will respect me."

"You are much too arrogant," she snapped.

"I know, which is why I'm so perfect," Samael retorted, loosening the tie just a touch. It gave him an air of insouciance that would show up well in pictures. "Did you bring her as I asked?"

"The girl is here, but I don't see why she needed to come. She's been irritating to deal with since Parker expired."

By expired, she meant the man had fallen to his death. It was quite the mystery—who pushed him? The cameras never did show a culprit. Nobody really cared, one megalomaniac's death not much of a tragedy.

"She can't be allowed to leave. Precious"— his nickname for her—"knows too much." Way too much. The secrets Sue-Ellen had learned over the years put her in danger. And not just from his enemies. *She can't be allowed to talk to anyone lest my secrets come out.*

"I agree she knows too much, which is why we should kill her. It's more foolproof."

"You will not kill my precious." He tugged at the sleeves of the jacket he'd just pulled on. "Nor will you allow anyone else to do so. And that also goes for harming her."

Anastasia tsked. "Now you sound like Parker. You are much too attached to the girl."

"Never fear, I won't let that get in the way of what must be done." While he held great affection for the gator girl, he had a destiny. So did she. She just didn't know it yet. "How goes the other part of our plan? I hear the treatments are mostly complete."

"Yes. We can proceed at any time." Anastasia smoothed the skirt of her red gown. Always with the red.

"What of Tomas and the child in his mate's belly?" A child implanted by Parker. Tomas, also a dragon but of the Obsidian Sept, had found himself enjoying Parker's hospitality for a while. During that time, his seed and special ability had been harnessed and used to fertilize a human woman's egg. A woman who'd been injected with something special and rare. In a few months, they would see if that and the other experiments bore fruit. So many exciting things about to happen. One step closer to ruling the world.

"The Mauves are keeping the couple closely guarded. From what we hear, Tomas isn't taking chances with his mate or his child. Our source inside the Mauve Sept says everything is progressing as it should."

"And what of the Silvers?" Via certain hidden channels, Parker's company—now Samael's company; a gift from Anastasia—had entered into negotiations with the matriarch. The pompous old dame showed an interest in a certain potion, which, according to very good rumor, she needed for a daughter. It was a potion only Samael could provide.

Anastasia flicked at his lapel. "The old hag is balking at the price. But she'll give in soon. She doesn't want a wyvern as a grandchild." None of the great families wanted a wyvern, which was the result of humans and dragons mixing.

Wyverns were the stunted version of dragons, incapable of fully ascending, and sterile to boot.

Until now.

I hold the secret to changing that.

He knew so many secrets, and tonight one of them would be revealed to the world. "Shall we go play our parts?" he asked the woman who'd spent her life— when he wasn't in the labs—

teaching him her version of the world. A world as seen by a dragon.

A world that is mine.

"This is not a game."

"I should hope not. We are talking about global domination. But, I should add, if it were a game"—he winked—"I'd win."

"It's time, milord. Priestess." Bertrand entered the room and immediately dropped to a knee with his head bowed. The man knew his place and respected it. Now if only he'd wear a bell so Samael could hear him coming because he certainly couldn't smell the man. Another annoying wyvern trait, but it made them excellent soldiers.

The wyverns of the Crimson Sept—a Sept that did not shun them as others did—served as part of their security team. They would lay down their lives for Samael—because, if they didn't, Anastasia would strip it from them.

"Outside doors are closed." From Bertrand's earpiece, Samael could hear the hum of voices as various teams reported. "Security is in position. The media representatives you requested have gathered."

"Then let us give them a story." Anastasia lifted her chin and strutted out. She didn't seem concerned at all about the bombshell they would unleash on the world. The woman who'd raised him had balls. Big ones.

But mine are bigger.

Samael knew how to time his entrance. He waited a moment before he followed. Let her prepare the way with an introduction.

Stepping up to the podium, Samael looked upon the crowd, all those human faces eager for a story. His story. And he gave it to them.

Time to make his claim on this world.

"I am Samael D'Ore. The rightful dragon king. The one foretold." What he didn't tell them yet was that he would one day soon rule them all.

And they could do nothing to stop it from coming.

Chapter Seven

The witch was coming.

Don't show fear. Sue-Ellen knew better than to let Anastasia see. Like most predators, Anastasia would leap upon any sign of weakness and exploit it.

In many ways, it reminded Sue-Ellen of Uncle Theo. Her dead uncle Theo. Good riddance. She'd worn a veil at the funeral so no one would see that she didn't cry.

Why would she? At least now her brothers were free. Her whole family was. So why was Sue-Ellen still here? Still dancing to someone else's tune?

Because Samael is here. Because he needed her. At least, he used to. Of late, she wondered if he really had any use for her at all.

What are you talking about? He wanted you here tonight.

The request for her presence was the first in a while. Pride screamed at her to say no. The same pride that kept her from calling her family to say she'd made a mistake and was coming home.

But where Samael was concerned, she had no shame. The call to join him came, and Sue-Ellen ran to be with Samael.

I am so pathetic. So pitiful that she didn't leave while he made her wait. Like a good girl, she bided her time in a room to the side of the stage, with hands clasped, the picture of demure obedience as Samael was paraded in front of a crowd.

How he must hate it. Sue-Ellen certainly hated all the times Parker had used her for the cameras.

"Smile," Uncle would say, the subtle threat in his tone clear. She smiled and pretended.

And no one ever noticed.

It was how she knew Samael's grin must be fake. He was just as much a prisoner as she had been, and his incarceration had started even younger.

According to her late uncle, Samael had been under the priestess's control since he was a child, whereas Sue-Ellen had been taken hostage by her uncle Theo only about six years ago.

Six years.

Six years of her life. Gone.

And for what? So Parker could use Sue-Ellen to keep her brothers in line. So he could dangle her in front of a wild-eyed Samael, who looked so hopeless in his restraints.

All those years, wasted. *I was used.* Used by an uncle who claimed she gave him the appearance of legitimacy. The doting uncle and his loving niece. Parker especially needed that image boost since his own children had stopped visiting after his wife suffered an unfortunate incident—also known as crossing Uncle Theo. They never did find her aunt's body. The car had sailed off that cliff into the ocean and had never been recovered. They had only a single eyewitness to tell the story—and the last known GPS coordinates of the onboard navigation system that confirmed it.

Now, with her uncle gone, shifters and dragons outed to the world, Sue-Ellen stood at a crossroads.

From this point on, everything will change. She knew it from the hush that suddenly settled over everything.

Creeping closer to the door, she peeked out to the larger room outside this one. The silence hung thickly in the air. She dared a peek. Samael stood before a small crowd, chin lifted with a haughtiness she didn't recognize.

Where had that come from? When?

He appeared tall and proud. A golden god for the people. A puppet for the evil priestess.

The man she'd fallen for six years ago.

He was also the one guy she could never have. Anastasia had made it quite clear that Samael was destined for greater things than the daughter of a swamp gator.

It didn't stop Sue-Ellen from dreaming.

It doesn't have to be a dream. The voice she heard wasn't hers. Funny how optimism sounded just like him.

She sighed, and Samael's head turned as if he'd heard it. His gaze caught hers. Green fire danced in the depths of his eyes. Most of the amber glow was gone now. Perhaps Parker had siphoned off too much with his experiments.

A lip quirked, and she could swear she heard

a whispered, *"Soon we'll be together, my precious."*

She should have been excited. Samael wanted her. He showed it every time they stole a kiss. Because of who and what he was, they had to hide their love for each other. Could only indulge in brief moments.

It kept her pure.

And very frustrated.

Did he feel the same frustration?

Sometimes, she wondered. They weren't together a lot, just the rare times when he visited, and those were closely guarded.

With your uncle dead, we won't have to hide anymore.

That was the message he'd sent less than a week ago, smuggled to her by the maid. A very nice note and yet he didn't explain how they'd get around Anastasia.

The priestess would fight hardest against them being together. Samael was too important to sully himself with a gator girl.

Given he was the only Gold dragon left of his kind, a Golden who was in his twenties now, there was pressure on poor Samael to reproduce. But his guardian didn't want just anyone to get his seed. Rumor had it Samael was about to get engaged—and not to Sue-Ellen. Even worse? She had a sneaky suspicion he would do nothing to stop it.

At times, it seemed like she knew everything about Samael, and yet, more and more, she felt as if she didn't know him at all.

Was everything he told me a lie? Once Parker

had released him from the medical dungeon, Samael began meeting her in secret. He told her, as they hid in abandoned rooms of the house, that he was the one foretold. Some big-shot dude in the dragon religion.

But this was where it got confusing because he often claimed he didn't know if he could handle the pressure. And yet, at other times, he bragged about how one day he would rule the world.

"I will make the decisions. I will set the rules, which means"—and he turned to her with an ardent gaze—"we can be together in the open."

When she was still a girl with rose-colored glasses, she believed it. But now, looking at him on stage, shoulders back, head held at a proud angle, she had to wonder.

Wonder if she ever really knew him at all.

Why do I stay? Parker wasn't here anymore to threaten her family. Brandon and Wes, actually *everyone* she still loved, had scattered when news of shifters existing came out. They saw which way the wind might blow and preferred to stay out of its reach.

Full humans had a tendency to overreact, and when that happened, people got shot, and shifters were susceptible to bullets, even the plain metal ones.

Sue-Ellen had remained for only one reason. For the boy she'd met years ago. The one she'd thought they tortured.

As it turned out, the one being tortured was her brother, and sometimes, at night, she still cried at what had happened to Brandon. And then she'd made it worse. When he'd come to save her, she'd sent him away. Turning her back on him had broken her heart. But Sue-Ellen's brother needed to move on. He deserved a chance at happiness when he escaped his curse of being a monster.

Now Sue-Ellen's dilemma was hers alone.

I should get out of here.

There was no reason to stay.

If she wasn't around, then Samael would be free to marry the right person. His people had waited so long for a Golden and an heir. A true heir. The only thing in the way was her.

The news conference ended abruptly, Samael bidding the media people a curt, "We're done," before turning and heading for her.

Sue-Ellen backed away from the door and clasped her hands, wishing she'd had this epiphany sooner and had practiced a speech. Then again, she'd thought about this before. She'd just lacked the guts to do it.

Not this time.

Samael entered, his smile wide. "Did you see how rapt their attention was?"

"Yes. You did well. But I am surprised to see you announced your existence. What happened to keeping it secret because of the danger?"

He waved a hand. "I don't fear danger. Besides, it was time. My enemies have begun to move against me."

"How can you have enemies when no one knew you existed?" That part of his conspiracy mindset never made any sense.

His smile lost some of its shine. "I thought

you would be happy for me."

"I am." She sighed. "But don't you see? Now that you've told everyone, it's more obvious than ever. We can't be together. It's time for me to leave."

"No."

She'd expected him to argue. "I know this is hard, Samael, but it's for the best. You need to move on. We both do."

"I plan to. However, I'm not done with you." The words emerged flat and hard.

"Well, I am. I'm leaving. And I'm going to ask that you not try and stop me."

He leaned against the door, blocking her exit. "You will go when I say you can go. I'm the one in charge here."

"Excuse me?" She'd seen Samael turn cold before, just never with her.

"I was really looking forward to our time together. Perhaps that will still happen, although I can't see the guards letting a prime piece like you go to waste." He shook his head. "And I can't stand sullied women."

"You're not making any sense." Sue-Ellen backed away from him, retreated until her back hit the wall. She needed it to hold herself up. "Just because I'm breaking up with you doesn't mean you get to punish me." Said with all the bravery she could muster, and yet fear soured her stomach. Samael did have the power. The power to do anything he liked it seemed.

"We can't break up because we were never a couple. You were never even a real choice."

"But those things you said…" The times he'd kissed her. Told her how he felt.

The laughter said it all. "You really are a gullible swamp girl, aren't you?" He opened the door and snapped his fingers. His ever-present bodyguards, with their disturbing lack of scent, approached, and the priestess followed them in.

Sue-Ellen aimed a pleading look at Anastasia. "Let me go. I did everything I was asked."

"Do you really expect me to release you?" The arched brow was carved perfection. "You know too much, girl. Just count yourself lucky that no one did this earlier. I've been advocating for your imprisonment for years."

"Take her below." Samael gave the order, and his guards closed in on her.

"Samael!" She turned a beseeching gaze on him. "Don't do this."

For a moment, his expression softened. "I won't let you come to harm, my precious."

She smiled, a wobbly expression, and managed a choked, "Thanks."

She shouldn't have wasted her breath. Instead of freeing her, he'd cemented her fate. "Take her, but I don't want her hurt." Hands grabbed at her arms. "Place her in one of the solitary cells. No one is to be allowed in but me and Dr. Michaels."

The Dr. Michaels? Samael hadn't gotten rid of him?

But he said he did. Said he killed him.

And she'd plastered him with kisses.

Rough fingers gripped her tightly, bruising her skin.

"No. You can't do this. Please, Samael." She couldn't help but beg, beseech the boy she'd fallen in love with. The one she'd stayed for. The one she'd given up everything for.

The one who now betrayed her.

He held up a hand. "Stop."

The guards carrying her halted, and Samael approached. Sue-Ellen bit her lip—too hard judging by the coppery taste of blood. Better she hurt than sob aloud in relief. She knew he couldn't hurt her.

Like Uncle Theo, he just wanted to scare her. It worked. She was terrified.

His fingers threaded through her hair, gripping the strands tight. "I never could resist you from the moment I first saw you." His mouth came down hard on hers, almost bruising her lips with the forceful mashing. She tried to find some measure of passion or thrill in his embrace, but all she felt was all-consuming fear.

Sharp teeth nipped at her lip, and she cried out at the pain. He shoved her away from him.

"This is how you beg for your life? Take her away."

Samael kept his word. He had her placed in a solitary cell, a prison where no one came to visit. Twice a day food would arrive, pushed through a slot.

A part of her wanted to ignore the sustenance, to curl into a ball and cry in a corner, but she wouldn't give in that easily.

She'd survived her uncle and his games.

She'd survive Samael, too.

By her reckoning, she had been imprisoned five days before he made an appearance.

It seemed unfair that he looked as handsome as ever. The tall, golden icon that all the dragons had been waiting for. Little did they know that they'd waited for a jerk.

She snapped at him when he entered her cell. But her human teeth didn't instill any fear.

She would have dearly loved to change shapes and really give him a good bite. But Uncle Theo had long ago suppressed her beast side. Something in the food made her other half slumber.

"Is that any way to greet me?" Samael chided. "I would have thought you'd have had time to rethink your attitude by now."

"My attitude?" She couldn't help an incredulous lilt. "Attitude is exactly what you should expect given that you locked me up."

"The cell was unavoidable, but you could show some gratitude that I didn't let the guards rape you."

"Excuse me?"

"Actually, the words I'm looking for are 'thank you.'"

"Thank you? Are you that delusional?" Sue-Ellen gaped at him. "I don't believe this. I don't believe you. To think I stuck around with my abusive uncle so that I could stay close to you." Her voice rose as her shame at her own actions tumbled out. "I stayed even though I knew Uncle was using my captivity against my brothers. I stayed for you!"

"And in return, I made sure nothing was

done to you. I told Parker you were mine."

Which sounded so good on the surface. So perfect. And yet, when Samael said it, she knew the dragon in him saw her only as a possession. Not a person. Not even a living thing. Just another trinket for his hoard. That was, after all, what dragons lived for, their treasure trove.

Her chin lifted. "I am not yours." She sneered. "I never will be. So you might as well kill me now if you don't plan to let me go because I won't be raped or used." She'd die first.

"It won't be rape. You'll be begging me for it soon enough. How long do you think it will take? How many days of staring at these walls before you're spreading your legs for me and pleading for me to take you?"

It would never happen. "For a supposed king, you're a douchebag."

Slap. His hand connected with her cheek. It stung, but she'd grown up with rough brothers and cousins. It might have been six years, but the tough bayou girl was still inside. That girl fought back.

Crack. The sound reverberated in the small room. She could almost hear its echo. It sounded an awful lot like, *stupid girl.*

Whack. His fist hit her, and she reeled from the blow. She knew the smart thing was to duck her head and apologize. She knew how this game was played.

But she was done playing nice.

So freaking done.

She wiped the blood from her lip and glared at him through her messy hair. "Is that your best shot? My little cousin hits harder than you."

"Arrrrrrrgh!" His scream of frustration bounced off the walls, and before she could blink, he'd grabbed her by the thin gown she wore and slammed her against the wall. He slammed her again and again, enough that her head rattled. Enough that she couldn't see straight. Her ears rang, and blackness crept.

Soon, soon she'd die, and she wouldn't have to worry about any of this anymore.

As if reading her mind, he stopped. He leaned in close and murmured, "Dying is too easy, my precious. I should leave you here. Forever. But that wouldn't be any fun. There's also the matter of your attitude. Disrespect won't be tolerated." Still holding on to her, he turned and dragged her to the door of her cell.

He yanked her through, ignoring the fact that she dragged her feet. Disregarded the pounding of her hands on his grip.

Where is he taking me?

She didn't like the angry set of Samael's jaw or the determined stride. She especially didn't like that he was dragging her the wrong way. Not toward the elevator and the freedom of the floors aboveground, but deeper into the place, to a door that required a palm print scan.

I lied. I'm not ready to die.

The hissing of seals breaking didn't reassure. Samael dragged her through, and the door slid shut, and she could hear the bolts sliding home.

Thunk. Thunk. Thunk.

Samael kept dragging her, and she stumbled

as best she could, but that task proved hard when he maneuvered the rough stone steps. The jagged rock that she scraped going down dug into skin as her thin robe—the medical kind that flapped open at the back—did little to protect her. As for her bare feet? Nothing covered them at all.

The stairs descended for a long time, lit by nothing, and yet Samael had no difficulties maneuvering.

Eventually, Sue-Ellen, too, could blink and see in the darkness. A faint luminescence let her discern things. Such as the soldiers ringing the outer walls. Armed with big guns. She saw a pit, a dark crater a few meters across.

A chasm crisscrossed with laser beams.

The type of pit that you threw bodies in if you never wanted them coming back out.

Sue-Ellen struggled in earnest, pulling and tugging and screaming.

"Samael, don't. Please. Don't do this." She wanted to be brave, but certain death had a way of destroying a person.

"Release the grid."

The beams over the pit wavered, and she noted that metal orbs, placed around the crevice, stopped glowing. What kind of shield was in this place? And was it to keep people out, or something in?

"Please." She begged one last time. "If you ever loved me, don't do this."

"Love is for the weak. Respect is everything. You should have heeded that lesson." Samael held her out over the empty space, his hands on her waist the only anchor to the world.

When he removed them, gravity accepted his offering. She plummeted with a shriek.

Chapter Eight

The noise woke him, which, given he didn't usually have to deal with noise—unless he generated it—grabbed his attention.

Did the surface dwellers not realize he napped?

He liked his naps. It was so nice to just relax. Not a care in the world. A very tiny controlled world with just one entity.

Me.

Boring.

Shut up. He had a voice inside him. It often argued, especially when he napped for a long while.

His longest slumber had lasted three days. He did so like to close his eyes and float. Especially after a large meal.

You need to stop fattening that ass.

Nothing wrong with the massive girth of his body. Size always mattered, and only small creatures claimed it didn't.

Then a bigger predator ate them.

They'd eaten Darwin, too, right after he spouted that obvious logic.

Are you going to do something?

Do what? There was that irritating inner voice, telling him to do stuff when all he wanted to do was shut his eyes again.

According to the plummeting shriek, his naptime was about to end.

With a jaw-cracking yawn, he rolled onto his back and opened an eye, only to have to quickly reach out to catch the falling object before it hit him in the face.

The shrill noise didn't stop. You'd think the creature he'd caught would be relieved that he'd stopped them from giving him a black eye or a bruised nose.

Nobody had respect anymore, especially not humans. He knew his history, even if he couldn't remember his childhood. Couldn't remember much more than his name.

He also remembered some vague rule being quoted as "Don't eat humans."

Probably because they were noisy and would taste sour.

The cacophony from the human he'd caught intensified into almost intelligible sobs. "Ohmygod. IthoughtIwouldsquish. Iamnotsquished. Ohmygod. WhyamInotsquished." Then, more slowly and thoughtfully, "Why does it smell like Uncle Fred down here?"

The babble almost made sense, and that kind of worried him. Had he finally lost his mind after all this time?

You are perfectly sane.

I am? Awesome. Good to know.

You are so sane that you know the right thing is to let me handle this.

Handle what? The human. He could handle

a mere human. Starting with gagging it maybe. It still talked, and smelled kind of rank.

Had humans stopped bathing again? The history books spoke of the ancient humans rarely letting soap and water scrub their skin.

Peasants.

Which, according to cookbooks, were quite delicious if roasted under the right conditions.

I don't eat humans.

Yet. He didn't fear trying new things.

Raising the captured human, he squinted via the tiniest slit at it. It had all the requisite parts. Two arms, two legs, a mop of hair. His massive hand wrapped around its waist, keeping it aloft but facing away.

Not that he could have truly deciphered anything distinct. The pit was dark. An abyss with no light.

What he saw appeared as shadows nesting within darkness. Very relaxing—until a human entered it and kept yapping.

It would take only a single twist.

Don't you dare. We should find out why the human was sent.

Good point. Usually, the humans that made it to his pit came dressed in sealed suits, armed with tranquilizers. He appreciated that they were bathed and ready for al fresco dining. Unless they peed. He wasn't crazy about marinated meat.

Not meat. Look properly.

Look at what? There wasn't much to see. Covering the dirty body, a shapeless gown, the type that gaped at the back. Pale skin peeked through in spots. Unmarked. Unseasoned.

No eating!

He ignored the mental shout and kept observing. The slender shape had plenty of curves, but it could have used a little more, especially if they'd sent it for lunch.

How can you think of eating when I know you're still full?

True, his stomach didn't grumble with hunger yet. He'd really enjoyed the fresh beef they'd dropped for him. Once he was done with it anyway—crispy on the outside, rare on the inside.

Delicious.

And quiet.

"Ohmygod, it's a giant eyeball!" she squeaked.

Yes, a she. Because the enemies of the nap wished to thwart him with the vilest punishment imaginable. A noisy female.

You won't win, enemies of the nap. I will go back to sleep.

He could and would ignore the shrill female, especially since she obviously did not recognize perfection. It insulted him so deeply.

More disturbing, why did the pitch of her voice tickle him with familiarity?

Do I know her?

She obviously didn't recognize him if she thought he was just one eyeball. He had two for starters.

Great big fucking eyeballs.

Check these out. He trilled in mirth as he opened his other lid, and she shrieked. "Fuck me.

You have two eyes."

Oh, look, the human could count. Could she also shut up? And what vulgarity. Ladies didn't cuss.

At this stage, can you afford to be picky?

His crazy inner voice might have a point. But he would not tolerate the caterwauling.

"Be quiet." He thought the words to her, not expecting much. Humans were usually deaf to his voice.

To his surprise, she stilled. Coincidence? *"Did you hear me?"*

"You spoke. How is it you can speak?" She whispered the words.

"Yes, I spoke. It's what evolved species do. And I will add, my kind has been doing it for a lot longer than yours."

"What are you?"

It didn't surprise him that she didn't know. His race did a good job of hiding themselves in plain sight. It made the revelation all the sweeter. *"Guess."* And while she thought about it, perhaps he'd figure out why something about her seemed familiar. It certainly wasn't her smell.

She smelled like a person shut in a box for too long without access to water. Very unappetizing.

But…fascinating.

It had been a while since he recalled anything interesting. Even that tuna they'd tossed down a while ago paled in comparison—and he'd loved the tuna. Big and raw, still smelling of the sea.

"How am I supposed to guess? It's freaking

pitch black down here except for your freakishly huge eyes."

"They are not freakish." Beautiful. Captivating. He'd seen them. He knew there was a long list of adjectives for them.

"Says the freak."

"Insulting me isn't in your best interest." He might have growled the words at her. And his inner voice laughed.

"Are you going to eat me? Because I'll warn you right now, I am sour."

"And noisy. I prefer quiet meals."

"Well excuse me for being alive."

He was taken aback by the sass. What fire. He might have chuckled, except in his current shape, it emerged more like a deep rumble. *"Why were you dropped on me?"*

"Who says anyone dropped me? Maybe I just thought it would be fun to skydive without a parachute down a hole and hope I hit something soft."

"I am not soft." He was made of strong stuff.

"If you say so, marshmallow."

Again, the urge to chuckle hit, and he exhaled sharply. His size diminished. As he relaxed, his other side took advantage, pulling with mental hands, trying to take control. Nope.

"Why are you really here?" Part of that question came from his other half. Sarcasm aside, she hadn't jumped, which meant the human had been sent down for a reason.

"This was my punishment for refusing to sleep with someone." She growled and peered upward. He could have told her not to bother. This shaft was sunk deep. So very, very deep.

And he loved it. He had absolutely no interest in the world out there. It had nothing he wanted.

Or does it? Every so often, a hazy image or phrase would hit him. He'd wonder for a moment where it came from. Then he'd nap again. Better to forget.

It's better down here. Quiet.

Alone.

Peaceful and relaxing.

Alone.

Shut up.

"Are you still there?"

"What kind of stupid question is that?" he asked with a hint of incredulity. *"You do realize you're still lying on me."*

"Hard to miss given you're quite large."

His chest swelled, causing her to slide. He caught her. *"Thank you."* Always nice when the humans recognized greatness. *"And now back to your abrupt arrival. You've invaded my space."*

"I didn't exactly have a choice."

"You did have a choice, but you let your morals get in the way. Perhaps you should rethink them."

"I might have been born on the wrong side of the swamp, but that doesn't make me loose."

The swamp? I used to love the stories about the bayou. The ones in those books. They arrived wrapped in brown paper full of vivid images. Passages were highlighted with notes in the margins. *Looks like Uncle Lou's place.* There was the house on stilts, swampy marsh underneath, with a boat tied to a wooden jetty. It said, *My idea of a perfect home.*

The elusive revelation floated through his thoughts, evocative and teasing because he couldn't recall who had given him the books. He couldn't remember anything.

And for the first time, he wondered why.

Why was his mind such a blank slate? A wealth of knowledge but nothing personal.

Until now.

Why does she sound so familiar?

Sound wasn't something he had down here. No television. No radio. Nothing to mar his serenity. He rolled to his side and sat up. This room was the closest one to his stash, big enough to allow this form.

"I take it you're not going to apologize?"

"For what?"

"Implying I was a whore."

"You made the claim. I just didn't argue."

"Dick. I hope you choke on me and die."

"I would rather starve than eat you. You smell."

"I don't care if you are the size of a whale. You're a jerk." A teeny tiny fist slammed him.

He was really beginning to wonder why he didn't eat her. At least then she'd be quiet.

And I'd be alone.

She lived for the moment.

He closed his eyes.

She stopped talking.

Fascinating. Snore.

Poke. He ignored the jab of her tiny finger.

Poke. Poke. "Open your eyes."

"I can't."

"Why not?"

"Because I'm sleeping."

"No you're not because you're talking to me."

"I will be sleeping as soon as you shut up." Did she not understand how this worked?

"But it's dark in here. Freakish as your eyes are, at least they light up."

"I am not your personal lamp service." Really, the effrontery boggled the mind. *"And since you're so unhappy—and vocal—about it, perhaps you should be on your way."*

"On my way where? Is there an exit?"

"I don't suppose you can climb?"

"Are we really going to pretend to be having this conversation? These arms don't do any kind of exercise apart from yoga."

"Are you always so sarcastic?"

"Yes."

He relaxed even more and shrank a bit. His other self was truly reeling in the reins, and he was having a hard time stopping him. There was something about this human… Something so strangely familiar.

"You are vexing. I can see how you ended up in here."

"Vexing is not a reason to throw a person in a pit with a giant, um… Elephant?"

She hesitated before saying it. That didn't lessen the blow.

"You are surely jesting." For one, he was much

larger.

"Well, you smell kind of dry, and your skin is scaled yet kind of leathery at the same time."

"My hide is the rarest you will find." And silky smooth, too, if stroked just right.

"Are you offended?" She laughed. "I didn't mean any of that in a bad way. You are just different."

Indeed he was—because there existed only one of him.

And only one of her. For some reason, that seemed important.

"Who are you?"

"The girl who made bad choices." She sighed. "Ever wish you could have a do-over?"

No.

But was that really the answer? How could he know when he remembered nothing?

Remember the promise.

What promise?

"You haven't said who you rejected." He could guess, though. Only one person he knew didn't handle the word *no* very well. From what he'd seen, Samael had no morals whatsoever. Then again, neither did he. It was why no one came down here anymore.

Because none ever returned to the top.

They should have left me alone. I no longer have anything I care about. Nothing they could truly threaten him with.

Wrong. There is one thing. He just couldn't remember what it was.

"Do you know Samael?" she asked.

A heavy snort shook him. *"Who do you think put me here?"*

Actually, it wasn't all Samael. Anastasia and that wolf pet of hers had a part in it, too. Once they realized they couldn't control him, they'd contained him.

But the only reason they can contain me is because I made a deal.

What deal?

There was an important reason he remained down here. Alone. Quietly doing nothing.

Had he mentioned alone?

Not anymore.

He set the woman on the ground, gently. No use tenderizing her flesh prematurely, especially since he'd not made up his mind about eating her.

Maybe she'd smell more appetizing after a good scrubbing.

Her hand reached out and tapped him in the lower belly. He allowed it because who didn't want to touch greatness?

It's why I touch myself.

But he hadn't in a long time. Short arms.

Still, an ability to masturbate wasn't a reason to let the other side take over.

Despite her claim to dislike him, the woman leaned close, close enough that he felt her shiver. "How can you live like this? In the dark with no room to move around?"

"I find this relaxing." So many things were better in the dark. His other senses had a chance to truly discern the world for him. Smell became key. Sounds, too. And feel. The way the air touched him

could tell him so much.

But sometimes those senses could blind him. Because, despite her familiarity, he couldn't place the woman.

Who. Is. She?

It nagged. So he peeked with his other sight, opening his eyes and filtering his eyelids so that he observed on a dimension that viewed the auras around living things.

She had none.

No aura. Just a smudge as if something covered it. Was her aura cloaked?

He heard a sniffle.

A hiccup.

Some other hitching sound.

What's this? The little human cried. *"Don't do that."*

"I can't help it." Hiccup. "I'm scared of the dark. Uncle used to put me in the dark when I wouldn't behave. Not a single piece of light, for hours on end." The soft admission hit him, and he frowned.

He might not know much, but he knew one thing. *"That's not a proper thing for an uncle to do."*

"My uncle wasn't a very proper man." She still hitched her words, and it bothered him that she would fear when in the presence of the greatest being there was.

"There is nothing to fear here."

"Isn't there? It's too dark for me to even see what you are."

Could she not smell his greatness? He could smell so many layers in her: anxiety, weariness, body odor in need of some chemical help. All of it, though, seemed to say—remember me.

My life for hers.

The words came to him and floated off just as quickly. They belonged in that dark hole that hid his memories.

The mere implication of the promise caused levels of adrenaline to spike. *She's dangerous to me.* He should have crushed her the moment she arrived. She was trouble. She was…

The reason I didn't fight.

The hand on his belly rubbed. "Is this all there is down here? Just a dark hole and you?" Tremulous, the words held such choking despair.

Pity welled in him. He was magnanimous enough to allow it, even though he shrank a little more. His time was coming to an end. *"If you insist on having some light, then move along the wall to your left. Enter the first tunnel and follow it."*

"Follow it where? Into another pit where I can fall to my death?"

"If I wanted you dead, I'd eat you."

"Great Uncle Herbert used to say the same thing. So one day, cousin Jorjie asked him if he ever ate someone for real."

"And? Did he?" He oddly wanted to know.

"Auntie whacked him with her purse before he could reply. So we never found out."

He only barely saw the lift and drop of her shoulders as she inched along the wall. It was fairly dark in here, even with all his special senses. She presented a moving shadow within a deeper cloak of darkness.

What was she really doing here? He didn't understand why she'd been sent. Did Samael want to trick him somehow? But then again, how would that work?

Samael had to know his first instinct would be to kill. It was why he was in this pit prison, after all.

Lack of cooperation.

Killing of staff.

He knew enough to know he was here because of choices he'd made. He even remembered some of the blood.

What he didn't remember was ever showing clemency. Why hadn't he let her splat? What if he'd not been in the pit at all? Would Samael still have tossed her?

All good questions, but the ones plaguing him most? Who was she, and why did he feel like he knew her?

She disappeared from sight into the smaller tunnel that wouldn't accommodate his current size.

I should follow.

Let her go. She'd be fine.

I need to know more about her.

Or he could have another nap.

He closed his eyes. Shut them tight. Took a few steady breaths.

La-di-da-di-da. Wonder what she is doing.

He didn't care.

Maybe she's touching our stuff.

Who cared? It was junk.

Perhaps she has some answers.

Maybe he should leave well enough alone.

There was probably a reason he couldn't remember.

It's time.

Time for what?

Stop arguing and take a break. A real break and let me drive for bit.

Fine. He could use a good nap.

He changed shape. Took all that lovely power and strength and compressed it into an itty-bitty two-legged body.

Argh. You're squishing me.

Go to sleep.

It felt good to be in charge again, especially since things had gotten rather interesting. He followed the girl, knowing the path so well he could walk it with his eyes closed. Today, though, he tread it with his eyes open, and the gradual lightening of the tunnel meant that his eyes slowly adjusted so that, when he entered the larger room, he could see his visitor more clearly.

He knew those eyes, that nose.

Forget. I am supposed to forget.

He didn't recognize the straw-pile hair and smell, but he knew that face.

Angel.

Who is angel?

Everything.

All his breath whooshed out in one sucker-punch as a very distinct memory surfaced.

It's her. She's really here. The angel who'd come to him so long ago. The woman who used to be the leverage to keep the beast contained. The one he'd bargained to forget.

And he had. Until now.

But now, she was in front of him. In the flesh.

Beautiful, lovely flesh.

His at last.

In that moment of recognition, her eyes widened. "You," she huffed, her eyes narrowed. "You bastard!"

Instead of running to throw her arms around him, she whirled and grabbed something and then, just as quickly, threw it.

He easily dodged the butter knife.

Something else came flying just behind, the three tines an insult to his prowess. "A fork?" That made him laugh.

Chapter Nine

How dare he laugh?

Sue-Ellen did the best with what she had. "You wouldn't be laughing if I'd hit you in the eye with that fork," she yelled. "Bastard."

What game did Samael play with her? Throwing her down here and having his pet catch her. Then sauntering in, naked and nonchalant.

"You would hold the method of my birth against me?" he asked.

"I hold everything against you." Her rage knew no bounds. Especially since he looked so freaking handsome. So perfect. So naked and ready to go.

Oh, hell no. "Put that thing away." She pointed at his package. "No means no!"

"You assume I have any interest in your odiferous body." He shook his head. "You overestimate your charms."

"You didn't mind my condition when you propositioned me in the cell."

"That wasn't me."

What? That made no sense. Of course it was him.

And yet...

It wasn't him.

This Samael—standing naked and proud—possessed a lean frame, much leaner than the man she knew.

That wasn't the only difference. His hair didn't have that perfectly cut and coiffed look Samael usually preferred. It hung past his shoulders, a long, shimmering, golden waterfall that curled at the tips.

Oh, fuck. This wasn't Samael. "Who are you?" she asked, and waited for that voice to speak in her mind again. For that velvety sensation to curl around her senses. Because she finally made the connection that this man before her was the beast from the cave.

He spoke, with his lips, and it proved just as nice to hear. "I'm Remiel."

"You must be related to Samael because, wow, the family resemblance." Visually, at least. But there was something about this version...something strangely compelling.

"We are brothers born of one mother, different fathers."

"Samael doesn't have a brother." Surely she would know. He would have told her.

Her own naivety slapped her because the proof of the lie stood before her.

Still quite naked.

She turned away, her cheeks heating. "Could you put some clothes on?"

"Why?"

"Because having your junk dangling is distracting."

"For you, perhaps. I'm quite comfortable.

And I might add, you're the one who dropped in uninvited to my home and proceeded to bombard me with questions."

"Home?" She couldn't help but crane to glance at him over her shoulder. "You live here?" She took in the space with its sparse furniture. The overstuffed chair, the material ripped in places, the stuffing bulging. The stack of paperbacks listed to the right that would soon join another that had already toppled.

By her side was a rock strewn with dishes, including the cutlery she'd tossed.

Her roving gaze stopped on the pile of blankets in a corner. "Is that where you sleep?"

"When in this shape, yes. The amenities leave something to be desired. Which is why I spend more time in the outer cave."

"But it's dark."

"Yes. And quiet. I have a feeling that's all over now."

"Are you blaming me?"

"The truth will set you free."

"The truth got me sent here," she grumbled.

"It's not as dire as you think."

Said him.

Yes, says me. The voice tickled her, and she gaped at his ass because he'd since turned away, displaying taut buttocks. The pale skin a testament to his molelike life.

Cheeks flaming, she dropped her eyes to look at her bare toes. Dirty, dusty toes.

Lovely. It didn't stop her from recalling his body. She wondered at the rapid pounding of her heart. Fear, surely. Nothing else. Attraction to Samael had gotten her into this mess. Attraction to his clone wouldn't help her cause.

Besides, there had to be a reason this replica of Samael resided in a closely guarded pit. No one went to this kind of trouble for nothing.

He's dangerous.

Yes. Keep him.

The cold thought came from the depths where her gator self was buried. Nothing else followed.

Uncle Parker had done his job of tamping down her beast all too well. The drugs were now a part of her.

"What do you know of Samael?" Remiel asked.

"Not much, apparently." Which made her want to slam her head against a wall and mutter "stupid" over and over.

"Given your shock at my appearance, I am going to assume my brother is still denying my existence?"

"Denying what? I never even heard a whisper that he had family. According to him, he's the last of his line."

"Not quite," the man called Remiel stated.

Her shoulders sagged. "I am such an idiot. I thought I knew him." But it turned out she'd been very wrong about that. So very, very wrong.

"Tell me, is my brother still playing puppet to Anastasia's games?"

"You know the priestess?" she asked sharply, once again turning around to peek.

He wore pants now, well-worn track pants that hung low on his lean hips. He sported defined abs and a vee that...

Her gaze jerked upward to his face.

A corner of his lip curled. "Don't stop on my account. Beauty such as mine should be admired."

"Not very modest, are you? Must be a family trait."

"We share a disturbing number of similarities. Except for one very big one."

"Is this a penis joke?" She'd grown up with boys. She'd heard her fair share.

"No joke, and stop distracting me. I asked you about Anastasia."

"And? How about you answer some questions first. Like, how do you know her?"

A single golden brow arched. "Are you seriously ordering me around?"

"It's called conversation."

"Feels more like an interrogation."

"You're making me want to bite you," she growled.

"Go ahead." He grinned.

She frowned. "This is the problem with not having my gator anymore. I can't strike the right note of fear."

"What do you mean, *anymore*? It is so hard to tell what you are over the smell."

"Thanks for noticing." She wrinkled her nose.

"Explain what you mean about your gator."

"I'm a shifter."

He frowned. "Doubtful since your scent is all wrong."

"Blame that on my uncle. Nothing like using family to test out new medical achievements."

"Is this a competition of cruel guardians? In my case, Anastasia was not related to either Samael or me, so she was quite diverse in her methods. No sentimental attachment. Especially to me. I was the difficult one."

"How long has she had you prisoner?" According to Samael, he'd known Anastasia all his life. But was that even true?

"My brother and I have had the pleasure of her acquaintance since birth. She is the one who orchestrated our hatching."

She blinked. "Did you say hatch? As in from an egg?"

The corner of his mouth lifted. "I did."

But she still had difficulty processing it. "People don't hatch from eggs." At his lifted brow, she backpedaled. "Well, we do, but not like eggs with shells. We're fertilized in the uterus. And grow there."

"That is how most humans and other entities handle it. But in the olden days, we chose to wear our majestic forms."

"And by majestic you mean?" Her eyes widened as she finally clued in on what he was. "You're a dragon."

"You say that as if it's a surprise. What did you think I was?"

Her lips quirked. "I guess not an elephant." At his glare, she smiled wider. "Sorry about that.

But cut me some slack. I've seen your kind but never gotten close enough to actually observe and smell one. Samael never showed me his. Said it was too dangerous. He didn't want the wrong people to know he existed."

"Probably because he's not as great as me." Spoken in a low mutter.

"If you're so great, why are you in a hole?" For some reason, she couldn't help herself. It was hard dealing with a guy who looked so much like Samael, who reminded her of her naivety. Now, if only her gaze would stop wandering.

"This abode is meant to keep me contained."

"Because you're a dragon. Given your size in the other room, I'm going to assume you ascended?"

"You know of the passage of a dragonling into dragonhood?"

"Yes, I know it. You told…" She trailed off. She had to remind herself that Remiel, this guy locked in a cave, didn't know her. Hadn't been the one to teach her anything. "I was pretty close to Samael before all of this, and he told me things. I also saw stuff."

Uncle Theo had done a good job of hiding his practices from the bigger world, but she'd lived with him, and Sue-Ellen couldn't help but catch glimpses of the events moving beneath the view of humanity. Hidden from everyone.

The world held more secrets than anyone realized. Secrets that would kill them in a heartbeat.

"My brother might have taught you some

things, but you obviously don't know it all," Remiel observed. "Or you would have known, in the old days, dragons wore their shape proudly. They hunted in it. Fed. Fucked. And eggs were how we created our young."

The vulgar word didn't throw her. She'd said much worse. "That seems so backwards. Didn't someone have to guard the egg all the time and keep it warm?"

"Someone did. That is what the lesser are for. To care for the eggs so that a powerful drake might fly the skies, his mate by his side, and keep dominion over their territory."

He made it sound so romantic. "Is this your way of that implying dragons are more evolved since they don't force the women to stay at home?"

"I am not implying. I am stating. We are more evolved."

"And arrogant."

"Thank you."

She almost smiled. "Lacking modesty, as well. Your knowledge is interesting. I've never heard Samael talk about this stuff or use the term drake." Sue-Ellen was fairly well versed, given that Samael had revealed so many dribs and drabs of the dragon secret in an effort to impress her.

In some ways, the dragons lived just like shifters. While violent predators by nature, they also hunted carefully. They took great pride in not getting caught. Samael had told her of the many laws, laws she recognized because the shapeshifters had adopted their own strict set to ensure they didn't succumb to their baser instincts.

It kept them safe. It meant their numbers thrived since humans no longer hunted them.

But the world changed. The various hidden groups, whose numbers had bloated over the years, grew restless. That restlessness turned into small spates of violent outbursts. The different groups grew less tolerant, especially once her uncle told the humans that monsters lived among them.

Now, every outed species wanted a piece of the different continents and even the oceans. Every side that had previously lived in hidden silence screamed just cause. They all wanted out of the shadows. None wanted to compromise. No one looked for middle ground.

A war was coming, and she didn't think anything would stop it.

Why would anyone ruin the fun?

The true predators of the world were tired of hiding. She could understand that feeling. There were times she wanted to loose her wild self. Go for a nice long swim in the bayou without a care in the world. Hunting for a fresh meal.

Instead, because of fear, she and the others kept themselves tightly bound, their other halves hidden.

Choking.

For a moment, she could almost see her gator rolling on her back and playing dead. How she missed the cold touch of her other half.

If only Sue-Ellen knew how to wake the beast.

Remiel stared at her, his head cocked to the side. Had he asked her something? Did she miss it?

Oops. Given Uncle's propensity for ranting, she'd developed a knack for tuning it out.

She tried a smile. "Sorry. You were saying?"

"Were you listening?"

She knew the answer to that. "Of course I was."

"Good, because I was saying we should have wild sex right now. You nodded your head."

Her mouth rounded. Had she truly missed all that? Was he really such a pig? "You did not. And even if you did, I would have never agreed."

"So you admit to not listening?"

She shrugged.

His lips pursed. "Way to crush my ego. You really were ignoring me." He sounded so incredulous.

Yeah, she was pretty proud of herself, too, because now that she paid him mind again, his naked upper body really distracted.

Thinking of cute kittens didn't help. Because she imagined them draped over Remiel like a blanket.

Way too cute.

Distraction. She needed distraction. "How long have you been down here?" If he said his whole life, she'd probably scream for him.

"According to the latest taunt by my brother, almost four years."

Four years? Not as long as expected, but still long enough to truly shock.

"Why did he put you here?"

"It wasn't Samael who put me here, actually. It was Anastasia and Parker's idea."

"Uncle Theo did this?"

"Your dear uncle apparently has a thing for putting people in dark places. I wouldn't obey anymore, and their drugs kind of wore off too quickly. I built up a resistance." His lips turned into a smile, but to Sue-Ellen, it fell flat. "They weren't ready to dispose of me, so they stuck me in a hole."

"That wasn't very nice." She couldn't help but feel sorry for him. He'd obviously suffered—just like his brother. "I can see why Samael chose to go the other way."

"You mean kiss ass and lick boots? Yeah, there's a real plan." He rolled his eyes. "Real males don't bow."

"He didn't have a choice." For some reason, she surged to his defense. "To protect me, he's had to do whatever Anastasia says."

"To protect you?" Said so incredulously. Did he not think her worthy of protection?

Remiel stared at her, his gaze pure gold, a dark gold that held her stare and tried to say something.

Something she wasn't ready to admit.

She turned to look around, realizing she'd still not figured out the source of light in here. Obviously, one existed because she could somehow see around her, and quite well, too. "Where's the light coming from?"

"The air itself. There's a gas in here—"

"Gas?" She grabbed her throat, feeling it constricting.

"A perfectly safe gas that reacts to the carbon dioxide exhalation, creating an ignition that doesn't burn but illuminates."

"So if we leave the room, it goes dark?"

"Eventually."

"If breathing lights it, then why was the other tunnel so dark?"

"The gas doesn't penetrate well through the side passageway, and the little that does, rises."

"You know an awful lot about this place."

"Four years, remember?"

Her nose wrinkled. "Don't remind me. How much longer do you figure they'll keep you here now that Parker is gone?"

"Gone? When did that happen?"

"A few weeks ago." She would have danced on the grave if given a chance.

"If he's gone, then the deal is in jeopardy. And the promise is broken." He said the cryptic words while pacing with a frown.

Odd—intriguing—man.

"How have you managed to live down here?" she asked, moving deeper into the room, toward a stack of books against a wall, the pile of them scattered like rubble at its base. They proved an eclectic mix of science, biology, and even government texts. Everything non-fiction.

"Do you read?" he asked.

The mundane question caught her off guard. "Yes, but not this serious stuff. I like fiction."

"Fiction isn't real. This is," he said, gesturing to the books.

"That's the mechanics of reality. I am more interested in learning about people."

He snorted. "People are overrated."

"Hence why you're a hermit."

"You say that so disparagingly, and yet I say communal gatherings are overrated. Society is annoying."

"So you're going to tell me you're happy down here? By yourself?"

His square jaw lifted. "More than happy. I'm finally at peace." He scowled. "Or I was until you fell onto me. Can't a man have a hole to himself?"

For some reason, this struck her as funny. Surely, there was something dirty in there somewhere. She snickered.

"What's so funny?"

She giggled harder.

He did his best to look stern.

She shrugged. "You said hole."

"I also said you landed on me."

"I did. Rode you like a cowgirl." She waved an arm around and yeehawed. He didn't seem impressed. "Do you not like a girl on top?" The scandalous words poured from her. She blamed a household of boys growing up. Six years since she'd hung with her family and friends, yet it seemed the bayou had left its mark.

It felt great letting it out.

"You are twisting things. I will note that, despite your innuendo, I was in control."

"Keep telling yourself that, sugar." She winked at him and laughed, but as she turned back to the wall, the giggles held an edge of hysteria. With reason. She was terrified. It struck her that she found herself stuck.

Down a hole.

A hole that had kept a man prisoner for years and counting.

A man that teased at her senses, sent her pulse fluttering and her heart racing.

I can't escape.

A glance around showed walls on all sides. And the ceiling overhead? It wasn't like the open pit with its high, gaping chasm. Here, it was only about twelve feet at the highest point, tons and tons of rock and dirt pressing down.

Pushing on this tiny bubble with me inside.

Panic suffused her. Did the rock groan with the weight? Were there cracks in the wall? She panted, and her head tossed from side to side.

"What's wrong with you?"

His voice came as if through a tunnel. Faint. Her vision narrowed, too. Closed in on a spot on the rocky wall. Rough-hewn. Where were the wood beams to support it?

It's going to collapse!

Chapter Ten

Angel collapsed! And in spite of her insults, he apparently felt obligated to catch her. Without even thinking, Remiel grabbed a cushion and tossed it the few feet needed, managing to have it land before her head could crack off the floor.

His angel had suffered some kind of episode. A panic attack, most likely. At times, Remiel fought the panic, too. A dragon was meant for open skies.

I made this choice. But one of the people he'd made the deal with was gone. Did that still bind him?

Sue-Ellen didn't remain unconscious for long. Her lashes fluttered, and she stared at him, eyes wide. He could feel the tension in her. Hear it in the short breaths she took.

"Calm yourself. You'll come to no harm."

"How can you know?"

"Because I'll keep you safe." He said the words, uttered the promise, and could have rapped his head off a wall. *What am I doing?*

He was falling into the same trap he'd fallen into years ago. The hole in his memories spilled images to him, enough that he knew who she was.

Sue-Ellen Mercer. Niece of Theo Parker. And

his damned kryptonite.

She still didn't get it. Still hadn't figured it out. Then again, it had taken him a moment, too. He'd done everything to forget her, given away everything he had in order to get magic that would let him forget.

The magic had stopped working. He remembered it all.

Remembered her.

He kept staring at his angel, noting how she'd matured. The roundness of her cheeks gone. Her hair a touch darker than when he'd first seen her, hair still dirty blonde in color but lacking the highlights of gold she'd sported in her late teens.

She obviously wasn't getting enough time outside given her pallor.

How he missed the rays of sun on his face.

She stared at him inquisitively.

His turn to blink stupidly as she gazed at him expectantly. She'd obviously asked him something.

"I wasn't paying attention." He didn't hide it.

"Just like your brother," she muttered.

Remiel took offense, took umbrage, especially since she obviously couldn't tell them apart. "I am nothing like Samael." For one, he was so much greater.

"If you say so. I don't really know you, and what I've seen so far isn't encouraging."

"Don't know me?" The claim angered him. He stalked toward her and noted how she held her ground even as the pulse at her neck fluttered.

Fragile in her rags and yet strong. Always so strong. So perfect. *And mine.* No wonder he'd tried to forget.

She held up a hand to stop him. "You can lose the attitude. I am beginning to understand you're not happy that I crashed your little loner pity party, but keep in mind this sucks for me, too. I didn't ask to get tossed down here, and I am freaking out about it. Have you seen how small this place is?" She hugged herself and shivered.

Was she cold? He took in her lack of clothing. The ragged medical gown she wore bothered him.

She would look much better naked.

"Did you just tell me to get naked?" Her eyes widened.

"Did I say that aloud?"

"Not happening."

"Is that a challenge?"

"This isn't happening." She moaned, tucking her head against her knees. She still sat on the floor, but on the cushion, legs crossed lotus style.

Remiel crouched in front of her. "It is not the end of the world." According to the seers back in his early teens, that was still about a decade or so away.

Then again, those same seers said he would rule the world, given where he'd ended up… Turned out they were wrong about which brother had a destiny.

"How can you be so calm?" She whispered the words against her knees, refusing to look at him.

Calm? He was a raging inferno. He just didn't know what he raged about.

He knew he didn't like her abject misery. No sadness allowed. She sat in the presence of greatness.

Prisoner.

A political prisoner, which meant he was too awesome for words.

"Give me your hand." He extended his.

She didn't grasp it. "How is that going to help?"

"Just give it to me."

"Why?" She eyed him suspiciously.

"Why must you argue? Just do as you're told, angel."

"Don't call me that. I'm no one's angel."

Yes she was. *My angel,* but apparently she hadn't yet realized it. "Give me your hand." He held his up, palm facing her.

"You're bossy," she claimed, and yet her hand rose and her fingers splayed. "I used to do this with Samael," she said, hesitating before his palm.

"Did you?" was the only warning he gave before pressing their hands together.

The shock of the contact saw her sucking in a breath. Her eyes widened. Her lips parted.

Hot damn. The spark was still there. Still just as shocking as ever.

Remiel had not felt it while in his dragon form; apparently, it needed skin-to-skin contact. It didn't help that his beast side went a little feral down here. All part of coping with the deal he'd made.

Because of that deal, he never thought to touch her again. That was the whole reason for forgetting.

But now, Sue-Ellen was here. His angel. *With me. In my cave. Forever.*

It seemed like heaven to him.

She ripped her hand from him. "No, this is not heaven. I can't live in this cave the rest of my life."

"But the spark? Did you not feel it when we touched?"

"Yes. And?"

"Don't you see?" Did he have to explain it? Judging by her crossed arms and blazing eyes, he did. "I am the one you saw being held captive. The one who used to call you angel. Not Samael."

A wry smile twisted her lips. "I figured that out already. I mean, it was kind of obvious, and I don't see what that has to do with living here for the rest of my probably short life."

"It's not so bad. It's quiet," he offered. He rather enjoyed the peace.

Or had.

Now that he had Sue-Ellen, he found himself rather liking the verbal sparring. It would be much better if they were both naked, though.

"Not so bad? You sleep on the floor." She pointed.

"Would you feel better if I said you could use me as your pillow?"

Her cheeks darkened as blood rushed to them. So his presence *did* affect her.

"What about food? I am not above eating

rodent, but I can't live on cave rats forever."

"No rats, I'm afraid. But they do send down crates of food every so often. Livestock, too. They might not want me rampaging on the surface, but they don't want me dying either. You never know if the priestess might have need of me." And the doctors weren't done with him yet.

"What does Anastasia want with you?" Sue-Ellen veered from the topic of them.

After everything he'd done for her, she thought she could distance herself. *Oh, no you don't, angel.* He didn't want to be far from her. On the contrary, he wanted to wear her like a second skin.

Figuratively, not literally.

"Anastasia wants what every dragon wants. Power. By controlling the return of a Golden king to the world, she is catapulted to the highest spot she could ever imagine. She wants to become the high priestess to the world."

"I'm surprised she didn't aim for queen."

"Queens are expected to bear heirs and be under close scrutiny. As priestess, she would actually wield more power, especially amongst the other cryptozoids inhabiting the world."

"Samael uses that word a lot. Although he shortens it to cryptos. He said he was expected to bring the Septs together under one rule. And then, once that was done, the rest of the world would follow."

"World domination is the ultimate prize for any dragon. It would mean the biggest hoard."

"Dragons and their hoards." She snorted.

"You should not mock the hoards."

"Says the man without one."

"Who says I don't have one?"

She cocked her head. "Do you? You admit to being a prisoner most of your life. Even now, I look around, and I don't see much."

"What makes you think this is where I keep it?"

"So you have a hoard? What's in it?"

"I can't say, but I will admit to having one. It was taken from me." He turned away from her and rummaged through the pile of folded clothes by the wall. He kept his small pile of garments off the ground. They sat on a rock, one of many standing as pillars and shelves.

"Are those folded by color?" She approached and touched the fabric, bumping her fingers over the stacked crisp creases. "OCD much?"

"When you can slow down and take each moment and use it to its fullest, you can achieve everything, including proper organization."

"Organization comes out of boredom."

"Don't tell me you're the type to leave things strewn around getting wrinkled."

"I also leave the cap off the toothpaste." She smiled, and he almost fell to his knees.

I never thought I'd see it again.

He found his balls and frowned. "How did I not know you were a slob?"

"Because if I only ever saw you when Uncle Parker was making a point, then that means we never talked much at all."

Because there was no reason to talk. He'd

felt the connection to her from day one—and she had, too.

He'd seen her cry for him, felt that rightness and possessiveness that said she was his.

She'd sent him little tokens during his incarceration. Books with notes. Special foods. Even a college football sweater that still held her scent.

She'd cared for him, the only person who ever did and wanted nothing in return. Which was why he might have snapped a bit when she said, "It's crazy knowing that the guy I used to make out with was Samael and not you."

She made out with my brother!

Bright, golden light flared brightly.

Chapter Eleven

Light flashed, something burned, and Sue-Ellen screamed. Any sane person would have when Remiel turned into a living torch that then transformed into a hulking dragon. A giant shape, like seriously dropped-in-a-vat-of-radioactive-goo mutant-sized, which meant he pushed against the ceiling, causing some of the looser bits to fall.

I am gonna die!

The certainty proved overpowering, and she dove to the floor, sobbing and covering her head with her hands.

She didn't react well when an object fell on her shoulder. In her defense, she thought it was part of the ceiling.

"Eeeek!" Total overreaction. Also, in her defense, she didn't know he'd touched her. She thrashed and screamed, which was how she found herself pinned under a man.

A very naked man.

"Get off," she gasped.

Stay on. The weight on top and all that skin felt rather nice in a twisted way.

What is wrong with me?

Why did she whine? She wasn't dead, and a hot guy was on top of her.

"If I move, are you going to start freaking out again?"

Possibly. So she lied. "I was not freaking out."

He stared.

"Much."

He kept staring.

"Okay, fine, I lost my mind. I'm over it now. Unless the ceiling really is collapsing, then I reserve the right to lose my ever-loving shit." The bayou in her came out, and she could have died.

His lips quirked. "We wouldn't want that to happen."

"No kidding." With her calmness restored, she waited for him to move off her.

He didn't.

"Ahem." She wiggled.

He wiggled back.

The O rounding her mouth couldn't be helped. "Is that…" She couldn't say it.

He pressed against her. "It is."

"*That* is wildly inappropriate."

"I agree."

"Then get off."

"I'd love to. But as for my position, I'm okay where I am."

She could tell. "This isn't helping your case."

"What case is that?"

"The one to get me to like you."

"I don't need to get you to like me." He smiled.

"That's not reassuring. Is this on the same lines as don't name your food?"

He laughed. "No. It's more about the fact that I don't need to make you like me because you already do."

"Do not."

"Would you like me to prove you wrong?"

Would she? Yes. Please.

His lips dropped down. *I think he's going to kiss me.*

Bad idea. So bad.

Do it.

With him so close, she couldn't exactly articulate why this was such a bad idea, nor could she stop him.

Don't stop him.

Before she could make up her mind, he'd bounded off her and strutted to the rock holding his neat piles of clothes.

This time, she didn't look away from the show.

Nice ass.

An ass he covered with pants. A shame.

Sighing, she lay flat on the floor and found her gaze rising to stare at the ceiling. She noted something reassuring.

"The ceiling didn't crack."

"This place is more solid than you think. They built it well."

"Built? You mean this cave isn't natural?" She'd assumed it was given its rough look.

"Dragon made, angel. A good portion of this place was fabricated or enlarged. Including the pit, this chamber, and a few of the others off it."

"There're more rooms?"

"Several more, as a matter of fact. You are looking upon the treasure room of an ancient Crimson matriarch. Empty now, which should come as no surprise. As soon as the hoard was discovered, it was stripped clean. I hear the dragon who used to own it had a penchant for vases. Pretty ugly ones. It was inside one of them that Parker found the maps."

"Map? What map? And what do you mean Uncle found it?" This was the first she'd heard of any map.

"Your uncle was the one who, more or less, orchestrated the events of my birth so many years ago. As a very young man, he came across the hoard hidden here by accident. He used some of its riches to buy the land it sat on. In that treasure was a message. A riddle that was a map. He deciphered enough to find the last Golden queen's hoard and the eggs in it."

Eggs. She bit her lip lest she giggle. "You weren't joking. You actually were hatched."

"Yes, and so was Samael."

At that, she frowned. "He never said anything about that." She'd also never thought to ask, assuming he'd lost his parents somehow to some tragedy.

"Does that surprise you about Parker? He was a man of many secrets. He also had lots of pride, which means he wasn't about to tell anyone he'd found a Golden hoard and then lost it because of a cave-in."

"Not lost anymore. It's been found again. By Samael. At least, I assume it's the same one."

"I doubt there are any others. What I do wonder, though, is if Samael and I are the only eggs they hatched."

Hatched eggs. Crazy plots. Experimentation and now a prisoner in a pit. "I can't do this anymore." Too much information bombarded her. The weight of all the lies pressed in on her. She closed her eyes and sighed, unable to look at Remiel because looking at him just reminded her of how stupid she was.

How could she have been so blind to everything? The lies. The half-truths. The fact that there were two boys, not one. How could she have not seen it? It seemed so obvious now.

The spark between her and Remiel still existed. A spark she'd never had with Samael.

I didn't care about the spark when he kissed me. She'd enjoyed it well enough. Cared for him, too.

He just wasn't the man she'd fallen for.

In truth, Remiel was the boy she'd stayed behind for. *He's the one who kept me here all these years.*

It should have made her feel close to him. Instead, shyness diverted her gaze and caused her tongue to stick. What could she say when she felt such guilt?

So much remorse.

Wasn't there a rule about girls who went from one brother to another?

Slut.

She didn't need her Aunt Betty's stark way of stating things to remind her. Remiel deserved better than a girl who couldn't tell them apart.

"I'm tired." So lethargic. She dragged herself

to the pile of blankets and collapsed on them. They smelled of him.

Of course they did. She flopped over and noted it wasn't awful. No lumps dug into her ribs. He had some kind of foam to cushion the worst of it.

The nest of bedding appeared more than big enough for two, and yet he settled himself close to her. As in right behind her body. His arm snaked around her waist. His breath fluttered her hair.

She didn't move, and yet that didn't stop heated awareness from flooding her. "What are you doing?"

"Going to bed."

"Can't you give me some space? I'm kind of having a moment."

"So am I."

"Not everything is about you."

"Actually, it is. I am the center of everyone's universe."

"You're not the center of mine," she grumbled.

"Yes, I am." Stated with such male assurance.

She wiggled, trying to move away. The arm anchoring her didn't let her budge an inch.

"Would you stop that?"

"Stop what? I am simply keeping you safe like I promised."

"Safe from what?"

"Predators."

"I thought you said this place had no rats."

"It doesn't on account that the snakes ate

them."

She stiffened. "Snakes?"

"Don't worry. They know better than to bother me."

"Is there anything else I need to know about this cave?"

"Caves. There're more than a few. Such as this room and the pit. That one is the only close one tall enough for me to really stretch out without breaking stuff."

"Why haven't you climbed out?"

"Do you really think they wouldn't take me out before I got to the top? Or have they moved the soldiers?"

She recalled the line of men ringing the hole. "No, and they've got a lot of guns. I can see why you'd prefer to hide."

He stiffened, and not below the belt. "I am not hiding. The guards might be well armed, but they are not insurmountable. However, you seem to forget if I made it to the top without being completely riddled with holes then there's that electrical grid to deal with. I don't know about you, but I'd rather not see if I smell like roasted chicken."

Mmm. Chicken. Now was not the time to think of food.

"Do all these excuses mean you've given up on escaping?" Because if he couldn't, what were her chances?

"Why escape? Think of it. What do I need from out there? I've got food. Books. A quiet place to call my own." He nuzzled his face into her hair and whispered, "You."

"You forgot something. You don't have me."

"I will." He said it with such confidence.

"You should worry less about getting in my pants and more about your freedom."

"Freedom to do what? Be hunted by the humans?"

"That hasn't happened." Yet. But she could see where it might if they got frightened enough.

"Actually, angel, it has happened. Parker delighted in having humans from the government come and poke at me. So many needles. So much blood. Not all of the puddles were mine."

"That's only a small subset of humanity. The majority wants to live in peace." Peace sounded mighty good to her right about now.

"Even if the humans left me alone, there's the other dragons."

"They don't like you?"

"I'm afraid they'd like me too much. Everyone has wanted to use me since I was but a babe still nursing. The blood of the last ruling Golden pair runs in my veins."

"So what?"

"What do you mean, so what? I am priceless to my people."

"Not really. I mean, why would they bother you when they have Samael?"

"Because Samael is not the heir."

"Really? Because according to Anastasia, he is, and they just declared on national media that he was the last Golden king."

He roared. "Lies!"

Chapter Twelve

Something agitated his brother.

A king shouldn't stoop to spying, and yet that was exactly what Samael did. He paced and watched the events in the mirror. *Magic mirror on my wall…*

Something out of a fairy tale and yet the only way he could spy on Remiel's cave network. Forget using drones. His brother ever did have a knack for finding and destroying them. The fact that Samael couldn't use technology meant he had to resort to other methods. More arcane ones.

Like scrying mirrors. The witches had enchanted many pairs of reflective items, random things that Remiel would never suspect, such as his spoons, the shaving mirror, the buckle on his belt.

It allowed Samael and the priestess to watch, but not hear. Watching, however, proved more than enough. Enough for him to see Remiel in bed with Sue-Ellen, not doing anything. Yet. "I don't like it."

"Like what, my king?" Said with the right tone of deference, and yet he could see Anastasia didn't really pay him any mind. The priestess with her red hair caught in a chignon and a loose robe that left nothing to the imagination was bent over a laptop. She spent a lot of time sending messages since Parker's death. Too many messages that she didn't let him see.

What is she hiding from me?

"Putting her with Remiel was a bad idea. I want her back." Because it burned to see his brother touching her.

Technically, he had her first.

So what?

From the moment Samael had seen Sue-Ellen—and understood what she meant to Remiel—he'd wanted her. The fact that he was told he couldn't have her by Parker and Anastasia only made her more appealing.

'Sue-Ellen isn't being prepared for you," they'd told him.

He didn't care what Parker's plans entailed. Samael wanted to claim her as a man claimed a woman. Wanted to plant his seed inside her womb and then flaunt her in front of his brother.

His desires were ignored. The Golden heir was denied because as Anastasia claimed, "Your seed is too valuable to waste on a swamp critter."

That was what Anastasia sneeringly called his precious. "Muck-born bitch and about as smart. Those kinds of girls are only good for one thing."

Anastasia was right. They were good for only one thing. Their genetics. More aptly, their eggs.

Sue-Ellen Mercer had excellent genetics for a dragon experiment. Anastasia was counting on it.

"You know you can't have her, and no amount of whining will change that," Anastasia reminded.

"I am not whining. I just don't see why I couldn't be first." First to breach her and then hand her off to his brother as a leftover.

"Because of the deal."

Ah, yes, the deal. The deal Remiel had made to keep Sue-Ellen safe. The one that Samael delighted in flouting every time he kissed her lips.

"He's got her now, and look. He doesn't even know what to do with her." The idiot slept— with his arm around her. And she allowed it!

"You have other things to worry about, my king." Anastasia guided him from the mirrored surface and pointed instead to a stack of reports.

Paper. Paper and more fucking paper. He was king, not a bloody secretary. "What is that?"

"Our spy network has been reporting their findings. Most of the Septs are showing positive interest in the resurrection of their Golden king."

"Who's resisting?" he asked, and yet he could have guessed the answer.

"Mauve and Silver. But they will come around."

"They'd better, or I'll crush them." He'd eradicate their line down to the last egg.

"Crushing the colors is what led to our decimation in the first place. You need to, instead, band the colors and any other cryptozoids under your banner. Otherwise, the humans will easily wipe us out again."

"We are not weak like our ancestors. We have and can use the same weapons the humans do against them."

"Have you forgotten how badly they

outnumber us?"

"They are sheep." He stood and banged a fist as he shouted it.

"Sheep who slaughtered their shepherds," Anastasia yelled back as she whirled on him, her eyes flashing with green fire. All dragons had the emerald flames when riled.

Except for one.

"We are stronger than we've ever been. They will not win." Not if they were more ruthless. Now that they'd found the ancient recipes, they would become even bigger and stronger.

Dragons would once again rule the world.

And Samael would show Anastasia who ruled them all.

He reached forward, lightning quick, and snared the priestess by the hair, drawing her close. Close enough that he could breathe against her lips. "We are no longer weak." He twisted his fist tighter in her locks.

The pain only excited her. "The king is mighty."

The king was. And the king showed her *how* mighty with his sword.

Chapter Thirteen

Sue-Ellen paced. Her world had been reduced to a rocky room. Stone walls. No windows. No air.

So much weight hanging overhead. No escape.

What if something happened? A fire or flood or...

Rumble.

An earthquake!

A sift of dust was the only warning she got before the rock overhead tumbled, crushing her. Squished her under its weight and—

Lips pressed against hers, halting the scream.

She blinked open her eyes and noted she wasn't dying.

Okay, maybe she was, though not by a cave-in, rather dying of shock because Remiel kissed her.

Kind of.

Not really. He just kept his mouth over hers.

"Whatareyoudoing?" she mumbled against his lips.

"They're watching."

"Who's watching?"

He didn't reply, just kept his mouth on hers, his hair falling in a silken curtain on either side.

No wonder I dreamed the roof caved in. His weight literally crushed. He'd thrown half his body on top of her, anchoring her with his bulk. The only thing separating them was a blanket.

Pity.

What is wrong with me?

Slut.

Stupid conscience.

She shoved at him, and he rolled to his side, and the disappointment was very real.

"How are they watching? Are there cameras?" She shifted her head to the side and eyed the walls with great suspicion.

"Not exactly. Do you believe in magic?"

Of all the things she'd expect a man to say, that wasn't one of them. "Depends on what you mean by magic. If you mean fairy godmother waving a wand, granting wishes, then no. But there are ways of harnessing forces." Great-grandma dabbled in the voodoo arts, and none of the granddaughters ever dared mock the dolls she made them. Not after cousin Daisy declared hers ugly and pulled out the yarn hair. She wore a wig to this day.

"No magic wands, but yes to magic mirrors."

"Great. Stuck in a hole in the ground and being spied on. This just keeps getting better and better." She sighed and flung an arm over her eyes. "I should have never left the swamp. My mother warned me the world wasn't a nice place."

"She was right."

"Thanks for rubbing it in."

"Are you always this grumpy in the

morning?"

"Are you always this annoying?" Actually, he wasn't. Their conversation was probably the only thing keeping her from curling into a ball and sobbing.

He moved away from her. She immediately felt colder and alone.

The revelation that he was the boy she'd stayed behind for, and not Samael, still confused her. Why was it she felt such a spark with him?

She opened her eyes as she sat up, noting the room still had the same dim lighting. The same rock walls. Everything remained as she recalled—unfortunately—minus one big man.

Where had Remiel gone?

Her first thought was that he'd returned to the pit room—the one she first landed in. He'd left her.

Alone.

That's what I wanted.

Not.

Dammit.

She hugged herself as she peered anxiously at the walls around her.

Did they bulge?

Did the pressure make it creak and want to crack?

Whimper.

Cowardice crept into her, gripping her with sharp fingers of irrational fear. Before it could completely paralyze, she swallowed any pride she still possessed and ran for the tunnel.

He has to be here somewhere.

And she needed him.

She bolted through the dark corridor, her bare feet scraping along smoothed rock, her hands reaching out to the walls to steady her frantic dash.

Popping out of the passageway, she found herself in the pit area, and her hands waved around in the wide space. An empty space or so it seemed. Who could tell in the darkness?

She couldn't even tell if she was alone. She didn't get a tingle of awareness. Did not hear a breath of sound.

She could only imagine the chasm overhead, the rock walls stretching high above, shrouded in veils of shadow.

Pressing.

Crushing.

Darkness.

In some ways, the void overhead was worse than the rock she could see.

All around was nothingness.

She sank to her knees.

This is it. I've reached the end of my limits.

How much more was she expected to handle? Why did life continue to be hard? Life continually betrayed her. Was it too much to ask for? If not a happily ever after, how about not being constantly spanked with bad luck?

For once, couldn't things go my way?

For once, couldn't she live without the fear and anxiety?

Sigh.

A hand fell on her shoulder. She'd not even known Remiel approached, and yet her body didn't react as it should.

A proper response would have involved shrieking and perhaps even ducking. Instead, she sighed again and leaned in to his touch.

Remiel was there to support her as she let herself relax. How did he do it? How did he make her feel safe?

Who cared?

"Why are you out here?" he asked, his arms braced around her, helping her to her feet.

"I went looking for you." Because he'd abandoned her, and for some reason, the very idea had demolished her.

"I simply chose to partake of the bathing chamber."

"The…what?" She stiffened and turned in his embrace. "Are you telling me there's a bathroom?" Because her bladder was calling, and she really didn't want to just pop a squat in a corner and let loose.

"More or less. I'll take you to it."

It turned out the bathing area was accessible from the main cave. The dark slash in the wall was covered by a tapestry that held in warm, steamy air.

Perspiration immediately formed on her skin. "It's hot in here."

"The cave I'm taking you to has some heated springs. They're good for bathing."

The tunnel, which, oddly enough, didn't scare her with him holding her hand, spilled into a glowing cave. By glowing, she meant the stalactites hanging from the ceiling and stalagmites jutting from the floor appeared to bounce colored light.

Red, blue, green. The colors rippled over stone, the kind of reflected glow that spoke of water. She could hear running liquid, the splash quite distinct.

It made her urge to go multiply. As in, cross-her-legs-and-hope-she-didn't-sneeze urgent.

He noticed.

How embarrassing.

"It's behind that big rock over there." He pointed to the jutting tower of stone that rose so high it touched the one from the ceiling and formed a pillar.

Trying to walk slowly, and with utmost nonchalance, when fighting a painful need to drop to her haunches and pee was hard. As the rock he'd designated got closer, her pace got faster. Just how big was this room?

She tucked around the boulder and quickly noted an actual toilet seat carved of wood sitting on some stacked stones, and toilet paper.

Praise a god she suddenly believed in!

She yanked up her gown and heaved a heavy sigh of relief. The constant tinkling sound of water served to act as a noise screen.

A much happier girl rejoined Remiel. She weaved through the short stalagmites on the floor, noting how they were shaped differently, the striations on each unique. All the stone formed a garden of rock and water, alien in many ways but quite beautiful.

But this underground wonder paled in comparison to the sight of Remiel, standing up to his waist in water.

Bare-chested, his long, blond hair spilling over his shoulders, he appeared a sea god rising from the depths.

All that strain to avoid peeing her underpants and she wet them anyways just looking at him.

Damn him for being so handsome. So familiar.

So painful.

She looked at him and saw Samael.

I thought I loved him.

She'd loved a lie.

But Remiel is real. He was the one she'd met first.

The one I really fell in love with.

Or did she simply fool herself again?

She wished her inner self would talk to her. Where was that voice of reason she'd gotten used to growing up? Why could she not have the advice of one who could smell a lie? She needed someone with her best interests at heart.

But her gator remained dormant. Sue-Ellen was alone.

"Are you going to join me or remain grubby?"

The temptation to bathe was huge. "I don't have any other clothes."

"That's a poor excuse. You know we can fabricate something with my items."

Good point, but she still couldn't do it, not when he watched. She angled her chin. "Turn around."

A very masculine grin emerged. "And miss

the show? I am only polite to a certain point."

"I am not getting naked for your entertainment or those watching."

"No one's watching."

"How can you be sure? You said they had magical ways of spying."

"They do, in the other room, but not in this place. I made sure of it. None of their enchanted objects are in here, so we have this room to ourselves." He patted the water beside him. "So come on in, and I'll scrub your back if you scrub mine."

She wanted to do more than scrub him clean. She wanted to rub her hands all over that smooth flesh and dirty it.

What is wrong with me?

She didn't strip, but she did join him.

He smiled. A devastating smile. A smile that crumpled when she said, "If we're alone, then it's a good time to plan our escape."

"Not going to happen. There's only one way out, and you'd never make it."

"So you've searched all the caves? Crawled through every crack."

"There's only one crack I'm interested in."

The wave of water she sent his way didn't make him sputter, but he did blink, moisture clinging to his lashes.

"If you're not going to take this seriously, then there is no point in talking to you." She turned her back and proceeded to submerge herself, sinking low into the water, letting the warmth of it relax her muscles. She closed her eyes and tried to think.

Think.

He's right behind me.

Concentrate.

What's he doing?

Need a plan.

I should plan to maul him for information.

Sigh.

She burst from the water, letting it sluice from her, feeling the grime of days leaving her skin.

"Now that you don't smell so bad, are you in a better mood?"

She rotated in the water that she might give Remiel a proper glare. "Have you always been this obnoxious?"

"Yes. See what you were missing out on?"

She did, actually. For all she shared a connection with Samael—and kisses—there was always a certain pomposity to him. He treated her like she was less than him.

Remiel in a sense did, too, but at the same time, he kept doing things that made her feel as if—

"Put me down!" she shrieked as he lifted her in the air.

"Not until you lose that serious face."

"This is a serious situation," she claimed, grasping at his wrists, lest he drop her.

"It is, and it can't be changed, so get used to it."

"What if I don't want to?"

"Then prepare for the consequences," he said before he tossed her!

Chapter Fourteen

In retrospect, he probably shouldn't have done that. Woman had this thing about being thrown, but her anger couldn't penetrate his wonder as he stared.

Once again, she stood from the water, soaking wet and sputtering, the gown clinging to every curve of her body.

Utterly beautiful.

So very tempting…if he ignored the anger sparking in her gaze.

"You jerk. I can't believe you did that."

"I'll do it again if you keep insisting we escape."

"You can't punish me for wanting out, and don't think you can stop me from looking."

"Look all you want. You won't find anything." Or so he assumed. He'd never really searched all that hard.

If there were an exit, would I take it? A day ago, he would have said no; he had everything he needed. What a delusion. Her arrival had changed everything. Especially now that he *remembered* everything.

"How many other caves are there?" she asked.

"Dozens, hundreds. The place is a catacomb of tunnels formed by shifting rock, dragonfire, and lava."

"Dragonfire? Is that a real thing?"

"Very. But not all dragons can do it. Each color has a different bend on their power. Fire is usually a Crimson Sept thing."

"And what about you? What's your super power?"

"I don't know." Lie. Ever since he'd ascended, he'd been practicing out of sight. Playing with his abilities and trying to hone them. It wasn't enough to own a weapon. He had to know how to wield it, too. He also needed to test its strength.

"Samael claims he can turn invisible. Some kind of deflection of light that allows him to move unnoticed."

Fascinating. Remiel hadn't managed that feat yet. "And you've seen him do this?"

"No. But, if he can, it might explain how my uncle fell from the balcony with no one around to push him."

"Parker deserved it."

"True."

"What else can Samael do?"

She shrugged. "I'm not sure. He didn't talk much about the shift. At the time, I didn't really care."

In other words, she was busy doing other things. He frowned. The jealousy burned hot. Anger, too.

He wanted to shake her for not realizing whom she'd placed her lips on. How could she not reject the touch of another?

The same way you rejected those Anastasia sent to seduce? his insidious conscience reminded.

A man had needs, and in his defense, he'd thought her gone from his life. She wasn't even a memory when those encounters had happened.

And yet, now, he felt such shame.

Then he mentally punched himself good and hard. He wasn't about to start feeling guilty. The fact remained that they were both ignorant of the truth.

What is the truth?

She's mine.

"Have you thought about using some of your super Golden powers to get out of here?"

"No, because not all of us are in a hurry to leave. I rather like it here." He didn't remember much of the outside world, having spent much of it in a lab, but he knew enough to realize it was fraught with danger for someone like him.

Danger sounds like fun.

Not as much fun as a long nap.

I wish someone would eat you.

His inner voice seemed a little testy.

"How many big chambers like this are there? Is the room I arrived in the only one with a shaft to the surface?"

"Why does it matter if there is another route or not? It's not as if you can travel them. You seem to have a dislike of close spaces, and there are many smaller areas than this."

She swallowed hard. "Smaller?" She straightened. "Whatever. I see what you're doing.

Trying to imply that I'm too scared to do it. Maybe I am." Her chin tilted. "But screw fear. If you won't help me find a way out, then I'll find it myself."

Such bravado. He quite enjoyed it. He found her crushing fear of before much harder to handle. She should fear real things, not intangible possibilities. Didn't she know fewer people died spelunking than those that flew?

"Go ahead and explore. I really don't care." He did care, but he wasn't about to mollycoddle. He wouldn't disrespect his angel like that. "Good luck finding a way out."

"That's it? Good luck?"

"How about send me a postcard if you do find a passageway out?"

Her brow knit. "And exactly what will you be doing while I'm being proactive?"

"Having a nap. Someone rudely interrupted my last one." He let the water buoy his body, and he floated. Eyes closed meant he couldn't avoid the wave of fluid washing over his face. He blew it out of his mouth porpoise-style.

"Asshat." Another wave of water got him up the nose. The snorting and coughing forced him to stand.

Feisty little brat.

Respecting her was one thing, but she took the sassy bit a bit too far.

I should remind her of who I am.

The sloshing of her steps meant she was almost out of the water when he looked. Looked and saw how her buttocks moved, slender in shape, the waist only a tiny indent, but he liked the lithe lines. It gave her a sinuous grace.

That's mine.

It sure was, but if he touched it, she just might tear his arm off. She didn't appear happy with him at the moment.

Let that anger give her the courage she needed to handle the caves.

"I can feel you staring," she sang over her shoulder. "Take a good look because it is the last time you'll see it."

"I wasn't looking." Lie. He screwed his eyes shut.

"Sure you weren't. See you later."

"Alligator," he said, continuing the rhyme.

No reply.

As a matter of fact, he couldn't sense her at all. Surely, she'd not left the chamber that quickly.

A rapid glance around showed not a trace of her. He exited the water and inhaled deeply, parsing the scents and noting hers—a lovely mix of so many colors—returning to his main housing area.

She hadn't gone far.

She'll be back.

No way would she go off on her own. He might have helped her find some of her courage, but a fear like hers wouldn't be able to handle the truly confining chasms and jagged, lava-bored holes.

He returned to the water to soak and relax, the picture of insouciance for when she returned.

Minutes ticked by. He counted them in his head.

Not back yet. Perhaps she lounged naked and waiting for him in bed.

Somehow, he didn't think that too likely. More likely, she'd chosen a tunnel to explore. There were a few branching out of the main chamber, hidden by more hanging tapestries. He hated drafts. His bargain with Anastasia for them was more than worth it.

It was dark in those tiny slits. Had angel found his stash of flashlights and batteries? For some reason, they kept sending them down, not realizing he didn't actually use them.

More time ticked by. Seconds that moved slower than flowing molasses.

So freaking slow.

And she didn't come back. His skin wrinkled, pruned into ragged ridges much like an old human.

She's not coming back.

At the realization, he finally strode from the water, a nubile god without anyone to admire him.

Eschewing a drying cloth, Remiel stomped back to his main habitat.

I am going after her.

No, he was going to have a proper nap. A quiet rest.

She didn't need him to save her.

Let her have an adventure, realize the futility of escape, and understand that they needed to make the best of their circumstances.

Yeah, tell her she's stuck because that's an awesome way to trap her.

It wasn't trapping.

You're not giving her a choice.

Fuck choice. He'd never gotten much

choice, unless shitty and shittier counted, so could these weak morals bugging him please fuck off?

Dragons didn't abide by the same compassion humans and other cryptos did. They were the center of everything.

I am the most important dragon in the world.

And yet, he was alone.

It didn't feel good.

Without the spell of forgetfulness, he remembered why he'd made the deal, the reason he'd finally given up.

And the basis for that appeared determined to abandon him.

Let her.

He didn't care.

He didn't care so much he took his time putting on pants. Took several moments to choose a shirt. But he rushed putting on his shoes and grabbing his knife.

A walk past a certain tapestry made him realize which tunnel she'd chosen to explore.

Snakes weren't the only dangerous things down here. And his angel had a mighty fear of—

Chapter Fifteen

"Spider!" Because, yes, shrieking the obvious aloud would so make her situation better.

Then again, how could it get any worse? The sticky web clung to her, and the more Sue-Ellen moved, the worse it got.

And I thought those skinny tunnels that I could barely scrape through were tough.

The tummy-clenching, body-sweating fear as she'd inched through those tight spaces proved less horrifying than the chittering sound that filled the room.

It was probably a good time to note that chittering sounds, especially combined with her current web situation, equaled a bad thing. A very bad thing. The thing she was most terrified of.

Spiders.

Don't mock. The swamp had some pretty nasty specimens. Cousin Felicia never did manage to find a husband after the biting incident on account of the swelling never going down.

No biting. Oh hell, no biting. Sue-Ellen couldn't help but shudder, and that only served to remind her of the situation. A girl stuck like a bug in a floor-to-ceiling web.

Stuck so well she could only slightly tilt her

head to see around her. The beam of the flashlight dangling from her hand cast more shadows than clarity. But the predator who owned this place didn't stick to the dark pockets.

Sue-Ellen was pretty sure the spider delighted in showing off its multi-jointed limb, popping it into clear view, the stark illumination highlighting the coarse hairs on the appendage.

Dear, Grandma. Please tell me you have a voodoo cure for this.

A leg that big and hairy meant…

Yeah. Really big, ugly spider.

Even more panty wetting? It wasn't alone according to the sudden tap on her shoulder.

She let out an epic scream. Like a real cavern-shaking one.

These arachnids apparently didn't have ears because they didn't suddenly go into paroxysms with blood streaming from orifices.

Shame. Because Sue-Ellen didn't have a backup plan. This wasn't a dream. She couldn't just pinch herself awake.

Nor could she count on rescue. Remiel seemed pretty clear he wouldn't help her. Even if he wanted to, she'd not told Remiel where she'd gone.

As if he'd come looking. She'd been nothing but mean to him. Now, she reaped the reward.

The web barely shivered as the first spider— Hairy-ella one—approached. The size of it almost made her heart stop.

Big couldn't even describe it.

Unnatural. Against nature's order. Seriously, nothing this grotesque and scary should exist.

As the tip of a claw slid across her abdomen, pausing a moment to poke a bit deeper at her belly, she really, really, really freaking hoped for a miracle.

A miracle named Remiel.

If you're listening, Remiel, I could use a hand.

Nothing.

Please.

Did he hear her? Did he approach even now? Timing his perfect attack.

The tip of the leg sliced at her shirt. Given her arms were stuck, it gaped open. "Perv. You must be a man."

The spider didn't reply but, instead, ran its claw over bare skin.

Remiel! She practically screamed his name. *I need you.*

Like now.

She closed her eyes and wondered how he'd enter. Probably running, with a can of bug spray in one hand and a lighter in the other. The whole web would ignite.

Hmmm. On second thought, no lighter, he'd just—

Slurmp. Something wet and slimy hit her, and she opened her eyes to see a gaping orifice still dripping goo. She'd rather not know if it was butt or mouth. Whatever it spat out was beyond gross and smelled rank.

It also made her gooey. On the brighter side, it didn't burn.

Yet.

"You're going to regret this," she huffed, fear bringing the fighting words.

As if to reply, another wad of goo was shot at her head. She managed to only barely miss getting it full in the face by yanking her head to the side. The painful tug on her hair made her suck in a breath.

Seriously. This is how I die? A virgin in a spider's nest?

So unfair.

Why aren't you doing something about it, then?

Why didn't she?

Because I'm as weak as a human.

Or am I? It's been weeks since Parker poisoned me. Weeks of not receiving that daily suppressant. But surely if her other side were awake, she would have seen signs?

I have heard her voice a time or two, I think.

Only a time or two? The thought was hers and yet wasn't.

Are you there?

I never left.

If her gator was there, then she wasn't helpless.

You weren't helpless before. You survived. Not everyone who dealt with Parker and Anastasia fared as well.

Just look at Remiel.

The poor guy. She'd blamed him. The victim.

Such an idiot.

The goo around her hardened, and several hairy legs began to poke at her. Way too many legs. The clack of mandibles was overkill considering her elevated level of terror.

Scared or not, she wouldn't give up. A

Mercer never gave up. A Mercer fought to the bitter end—and cheated if they could.

Facing the many-faceted unblinking stare of the ugliest spider she'd ever seen, Sue-Ellen growled, "*Hasta la vista*, spidies!"

It was an awful *Terminator*/Arnold impression, but it served as a focal point for her will. The will she needed to become something else.

Something great and primal.

Digging her hands deep into the sleeping pit within her mind, she grabbed at her beast. The gator's essence proved heavy and sluggish. How she missed the ease she'd once taken for granted. Once upon a time, she used to easily slip in and out of her shape.

Come on, big girl. She tugged on her sleeping gator. *Let's go play.*

The other half of her began to move in the right direction, slipping into the cracks that were needed to control.

That's a good girl. Come on, we have to do this. She cajoled her beast, knowing the time grew short, and still, her gator proved reluctant.

So it might be a good time to tell you…

Tell me what, she asked herself, trying to not growl in impatience.

Things have changed since the last time you saw me.

Changed how? And it did matter? They wouldn't survive the next hour if her gator didn't act.

Don't say I didn't warn you.

With a sudden surge of strange power—stranger than Sue-Ellen recalled—her other half took over, and she morphed.

Body and limbs reshaping, the joints adjusting, the muscles thickening, her skin hardening into a more leathery countenance. Her change pushed at the goo, and even dissolved parts of it. The steaming stench actually proved quite pleasant.

Weirdest thing.

Lips curved, and her eyes fell to a half hood as an odd euphoria relaxed her limbs.

I suddenly feel a hell of a lot better. Stronger, too. She smiled as she easily tore at the remaining web and stood.

Stood? That was new. Since when could her gator manage to balance on its two tiny back legs?

Then again… She looked down. *I don't think I'm a gator.* Her limbs looked rather long still, and green.

Most of her still looked pretty much Sue-Ellen shaped; it just wasn't a gator. Not even close, because gators didn't have wings.

"What the fu—" She never finished the curse because something hissed, and a sharp-tipped leg stabbed.

Oh, hell no. She dodged, her reflexes so fast in this shape. Fast enough that she managed to whirl and grip the leg.

Yank.

Tear.

A shriek.

A smile because now Sue-Ellen was armed. A giant swing and she knocked a few more limbs askew, which caused a bit of consternation.

Time to play. She propped the leg on her shoulder and said, "Let's go, biatches!"

Then she worked out a bit of frustration, and for the curious, she was quite good at it.

See the thing about growing up with brothers was that Sue-Ellen knew how to defend herself. She just didn't usually win, mostly because her brothers were giants compared to her. That wasn't a problem with these unacceptable affronts of nature.

Her new shape gave her speed and strength. Add in a whole lot of anger issues, and she had a never-ending fuel for it. Her frustration started with Samael.

"Lie to me about being his brother, will he," she huffed as the leg she held jabbed at a freaky eye.

Squish.

Squeee!

"What a no-good jerk!" she huffed. But then again, was Remiel that much better? "Misogynistic pig. Telling me I have to be with him forever. Ha." Swish. "I'll be the one deciding that." Slash.

And still on the thread of Remiel. "I can't believe he won't even try to escape."

Rip.

She dangled her fresh weapon and addressed the now much-less-legged spider. "Then again, some would say it is flattering that he wants to stay here with me."

A random thought hit her, and she scowled. "But does he want me only because he doesn't have any other prospects?"

For a man who didn't exactly have his

choice in women, he certainly had no problem putting her off.

As she mulled this point, the spider tried to retreat, but she lunged and grabbed it by a hairy leg. "Oh, hell no. You're not going yet. I am not done dealing with my issues."

The arachnid yanked and sacrificed another leg before scurrying off. His poor companion lay on the floor unmoving.

Remiel chose that moment to enter and looked at the body, her, and the pile of legs strewn around her.

"About time you arrived," she snapped, the words sounding strange with her forked tongue.

"Did you miss me?"

"No!" Yes. She glared.

His nose wrinkled. "You need another bath."

She threw the leg in spear-like fashion at his head.

Chapter Sixteen

"Fffuck you! Ssstupid man." Her words lisped since her split tongue had to pronounce the English words differently. He thought it cute, if a tad vulgar.

"Now, now, angel, there's no need to be rude."

"You got here too late."

"How do you figure since we never set a time to meet?"

"I needed you."

"I've been here awhile. I didn't want to interrupt."

"I could have usssed a hand."

"Doesn't look like it to me." He made a point of looking at the gore on the floor. "And I wasn't about to be accused of sexism. Anything I can do, you can do, too."

"The expression isss I can do better." Said with an angry lisp.

"Now you're just being silly."

"Don't you dare patronize me. Forget what I said. I didn't need you. I had the situation perfectly under control." The more she spoke, the more her words emerged as they should.

"You think you had this covered? Does this

mean I should have left the ones outside alone?"

Her nostrils flared. "There are more?"

He smiled, that of a predator who'd made the kill. "Not anymore."

"Well, they can't have been that bad since you took care of them without getting dirty." She cast a disdainful gaze on his clothing.

Princessss.

He could have sworn he heard the lisped snicker in his mind—but it wasn't his voice.

She waved a hand at him. "Take off your ssshirt and turn around."

"Why?"

"Give me your ssshirt." She held out her hand.

"But you're filthy."

She glared.

The heat of it only served to warm his recently sluggish blood. He wondered how hot her stare could get. "And smelly."

"Don't make me kill you," she growled. "It'sss been a rough day."

"Hey, don't blame me," he said, pulling off his shirt. "I told you not to go exploring." He tossed it to her before turning around. Antagonizing her more at this point could be dangerous for his health.

"You." Pause. "Are." The pitch of the voice changed. "The most annoying man." The dulcet tones of his angel returned.

"I am not annoying. You just don't have the right respect for someone of my stature."

"Respect? I'd have a higher opinion of you if

you weren't a coward napping in your cave."

Coward? He drew himself tall. "I am not afraid of anything."

"Yes, you are. Otherwise, why would you hide down here? And before you answer, yes, you are hiding."

"You don't understand."

"Then tell me."

"I will not be ordered."

"Why won't you tell me?"

"Why did you stay?" He turned the tables on her. "You weren't held in a cage. You had the run of the upper world. Why didn't you flee? Hide?" Because had she left, then perhaps he could have, too.

"I stayed for you." She bit her lip. "At least, at first I did. I wanted to save you." Her shoulders drooped. "And yet, I couldn't."

Vicious circle. Because she didn't leave, Parker had used Sue-Ellen against Remiel. But that wasn't her fault. Who could have known how much she'd mean to him?

"So you stayed to rescue me, and then you were too busy making googly eyes at my brother, I'll wager, to even think of running."

"Don't make it sound like that."

"Like what? Like you wanted to be with him?"

"Because I thought he was you. And do you know what sucks about that? Do you?" She'd gotten close as she yelled at him, close enough she could poke him in the chest. "What sucks is, right off the hop, I knew there was something off about

Samael. Something that didn't feel right. But at that point, I felt I had to try with him because I had given up my life for you."

What a coincidence since he'd given up his. She just didn't know it.

He reached out for her, snaring her around the waist and drawing her close, close enough that his own shirt brushed his skin, and the rancid smell of dead spider made the moment a miasmic challenge.

"I would kiss you right now, but…"

"But what?" she said, her eyes half-shuttered, her lips parted.

"You really smell."

"Argh!" She punched him. Not hard enough to hurt. She also began ranting again. "I hate you. You obviously never needed me, and I don't need you. So why don't you go back to your little cave, and I'll go find a way out even if I have to dig!"

Despite her ranting to the contrary, Remiel could tell she didn't mean it. She was happy he'd come to find her. He couldn't blame her. On a scale of one to ten for awesome, Remiel ranked pretty high.

As a matter of fact, he was so awesome that, despite her vehement exclamation that she could walk—and ignoring her silly threat to chop off his manparts—he threw her over his shoulder, sacrificing his clean skin to the spider guts still hanging off her, and led her back to the hot springs.

She kept ranting. He let her. Hearing it meant she'd emerged safely from her adventure, but it was close.

It had been some time since he'd cleaned out this section of tunnels for sport. Time enough that the arachnid colony had grown quite large. Obviously pooling their strength and numbers until they could attack en masse.

He appreciated that she'd triggered the trap by offering herself as bait. While she kept the king and queen of the spiders busy, he'd taken care of the swarm of youngsters waiting in the halls for dinner.

What he'd not expected when he'd finally come to check on her was to see her walking on two legs while in a hybrid shape.

"So what's up with your shifter side? I thought you were a gator?" he asked because, perhaps he was just a poor dumb lab dragon, but weren't gators long and narrow creatures, with short limbs, long snouts, and oh yeah, no wings!

Sue-Ellen had wings. Pretty big ones, too. She looked more wyvern than gator. *But she smells like...* Surely, he imagined any familiarity.

"I am a freaking gator. Or at least I used to be. I don't know what the fuck I was back in that cave."

"I take it this is the first time you've sprouted wings."

"Yes, and walked on two legs. Legs! I even had boobs."

While the boob comment really deserved exploration, he kept the topic on the more serious matter at hand. "Did your uncle experiment on you?"

"A little. According to him, he didn't really

want much done to me because he wanted to keep my blood and other genes pure. Apparently, the Mercer line has excellent genetics for experiments. So he kept mine clean other than the drugs he used to keep my other side suppressed."

"He did more than suppress it. He changed you."

She no longer seemed as surprised and mused aloud, "Just like he changed my brother, Brandon."

"What did he do to your brother?" It took her a few moments of him carrying her back through the tunnels to the main ones he lived in for her to recount what had happened to Brandon.

In a nutshell, Parker had injected him with certain genetic traits, and they'd stuck. Brandon became what they called a flying lizard man. But it turned out Brandon was more than that. He was dragon, what they called an unascended dragon. Kind of like a wyvern, but cooler. The amazing part of the story, though, wasn't Parker's ability to so thoroughly change the genetic makeup of a shifter, but the fact that he'd managed to actually change a gator into a dragon.

Which, of course, led to Sue-Ellen asking him as he put her down on her feet, her arms crossed over her chest, "Does the fact that I've got wings mean I'm also a dragon?"

He shrugged. "I don't know."

"What do you mean you don't know? Can't you smell these things or something? It's not like I can smell myself."

"I can't smell you either under that stink."

Her eyes narrowed. "I get it. I need a bath," she snapped, walking into the water. She kept the shirt on at first, the water soaking it translucent. It clung to her frame for a moment before she pulled it off and tossed it to the side, letting it float along the surface.

The temptation to join her proved fierce. Common sense said she wasn't quite ready for him. Common sense really needed a kick in the ass.

"Don't forget to use soap."

She presented him a middle finger salute, and he laughed. He also stripped so he could wade in after her.

She went out far enough that the water came to her mid-chest. Under she went, completely submerging herself.

He couldn't help himself from moving closer to her and sinking below the surface, and not just because of the gore coating him.

She drew him.

Angel was a bright and shining treasure that screamed, *I have a future.*

Now if only she felt it, too.

What was with her obsession about escape? They were in an underground cave network with hot springs.

Alone.

He'd graced her with his epic nakedness.

She blessed him with her even more awesome nudity.

They were both clean. So deliciously clean.

Why would they escape? Did she not see what a perfect world they could have together down here? Just him and his angel. They could build a serene life, one without outsiders trying to mess it up.

Perhaps she needed to see the benefits. He could get her some luxuries. As for how he would pay...

Anastasia would cream her panties when she found out Remiel was ready to negotiate some of his extra-special essence to get treats like a proper mattress. Some dresses. A maid's uniform with a garter. A mixer so Sue-Ellen could make him cakes.

He'd make this into a perfect home for her. He just had to make her believe it started with squashing her plans. "We can't escape."

"Can't?" She arched a brow. "That seems pretty absolute."

"Because it is."

"Have you even tried? I mean, I was able to travel miles today"—in reality about the length of a football field—"and there were still tons of tunnels left to explore."

"The place is honeycombed with them. Maybe eventually you'd get out, but why would you go through the trouble?"

"Because normal people don't live in caves."

In retrospect, "Don't worry, you'll get used to it," was probably not the reply she was looking for.

In his defense, all the blood in his head rushed south when she turned in the water. She'd risen from the depths, a wet nymph with skin softer than anything, the arm over her breasts only just hiding them, the curves still peeking.

She was so beautiful, and he worshipped her with his gaze. Bathed her with his ardent admiration.

She snapped her fingers. "Are you hearing a word of what I'm saying?" She sounded a touch terse.

He had a cure for that. It would help them both. "Did anything you say involve your mouth on my body?"

"No."

"My mouth on yours?"

"No."

"Then, I have no idea what you said, and I don't really care." He truly didn't. She addled all his wits.

"You are such a man!"

"Yes." About time she noticed.

"That wasn't a compliment." Said with a grumble, but she couldn't hide the flush in her cheeks. "We need to make a plan to get out of here. I can't stay, Remiel." She cast a glance around and shivered before hugging herself. "I just can't."

Looking at her pale features, the fear in them quite stark, it hit him.

She's right. We have to go. She belongs in the sunshine, with all the fresh scents that entailed.

Sue-Ellen deserved only the best, and it was his job, nay, his *duty* to give it to her.

There are so many things she deserves, and I should be the one to deliver.

And he meant that in the dirtiest way possible.

"I'll get you out."

"Do you mean it?" The hope in her eyes was worth any effort.

"Yes. I am a man of my word."

"Thank you."

"How thankful are you?" He snaked an arm around her waist and drew her close.

She gasped. "What are you doing?"

Doing what he should have done the first moment he'd seen her. "Sealing the deal." He dipped his head and kissed her, a real kiss this time. A meeting of lips, hers soft and pliant to his hard ones.

She didn't pull away. She parted her lips, and he felt the warm huff of her breath. Her essence entered him. He felt it touch him, invade him.

He welcomed it. He let the tip of his tongue taste the inside of her mouth. She made a noise, a small grunt of pleasure.

He squeezed her, perhaps a touch too tightly.

"Easy there," she said with a soft laugh.

"I'll have to remember to be careful with you."

"You say that like we're going to be together for a while, but we're getting out of here, aren't we?"

"That is part of the deal, yes."

"Once we escape, you'll be able to date whoever you like. I highly doubt you'll want to stick with a swamp girl."

"You are more than a gator now, angel. I've seen your new shape."

"Thanks for the reminder I'm a freak while

you're a dragon."

"What part of I don't care do you not grasp?"

"The part that says no matter what you want, they will never allow it."

"You think they can tell me what to do? I'm a prisoner, held by my own kind. If I escape, do you really think I'll give a damn about their rules?" He leaned toward her, and he could feel the fire in him burning bright. He wondered if it appeared in his eyes. "I will do as I damned well please."

"You can do better."

"I want you. I've wanted you since the first time I set eyes on you. So, get used to it. Sticking together is part of the deal."

"What deal? I didn't agree to anything."

That was what she thought. She'd soon learn. "The deal is I get you out of this prison, and you'll stay with me forever and ever."

A furrow crossed her brow. "Are you asking me to marry you?"

Ask? Snort. "More like telling. We shall marry. Or mate. Call it whatever you like. We'll do some kind of legal bonding ceremony to ensure there is no question as to whom you belong to."

"You want to marry me." She seemed to be having a hard time with the concept.

"Yes, although it's just a formality given your status already."

"What status?"

"As my hoard."

"What hoard? I thought you said they took yours."

"They did. But now I have it back."

She blinked. Shook her head. "I'm lost. Or I must be misunderstanding because I think you just implied I am part of your hoard."

"Not part of. You *are* my hoard. The only thing of worth that I ever had. The only thing I ever want."

It was an admission that he expected would floor her. Surely she understood the great honor he paid her.

Instead, she slapped him and walked away.

Chapter Seventeen

Tears burned in her eyes at his raw admission.

I am so unworthy of him.

Yet Remiel saw Sue-Ellen as the sum of everything.

It was the ultimate flattery—and the most frightening thing ever.

She knew enough about dragons to know what kind of stock they put in their hoard. Most dragons tended to gravitate to one thing they needed to collect above all else. Some collected old coins. Samael was obsessed with the original Dungeons and Dragons books.

But Remiel? He had only her. Boy did he get screwed.

Bull crap. Her mother hadn't raised a moron. Men would say anything for sex. He just said what he did to try and get in her pants.

Pants? Hold on a second, she wasn't wearing any. Or a shirt.

She froze midstep and thus didn't miss the drawled, "Nice ass."

Her cheeks burned, and she wished for something to cover herself.

Why?

He liked what he saw? Then let him look.

Giving her hair a shake, she set off walking again, hips swinging.

She'd no sooner ducked through the curtain leading to the main chamber than Remiel was on her, his body wrapping around hers. Somehow, he got her to the makeshift bed, hiding her under the blankets.

"Did you forget about the watchers?" he hissed.

Actually, she had, but of more interest was his reaction. He'd shown jealousy. Sweet, hot jealousy.

The knowledge proved heady—and arousing. But she couldn't let it distract her. Couldn't let it sway her path.

She should use this opportunity and hope that Samael watched. Would he feel jealous, too?

To make sure, she looped her arms around Remiel's neck and drew him down.

He grumbled. "What are you doing?"

"Shh, sugar. Just play along," her lips whispered against his.

"Play at what?"

His body effectively covered her. Skin to skin. Scorching hot skin. Dear God, so much flesh touching hers. Her body heated. She tingled as arousal swept her body.

But she needed to continue with her plan, the plan to grab Samael's attention. She nuzzled Remiel's cheek, inhaling his scent. "Relax and pretend you're enjoying yourself. It's part of the plan."

"What plan?" he asked through gritted teeth. "To drive me crazy?"

"Am I?" She wiggled against him. She could feel the proof of his desire pressing hotly against her.

"I've been waiting for this moment forever."

"Whereas I thought I was getting my moment." She sighed against his lips. "I'm sorry I didn't know the difference."

"Can you tell it now?" he asked, giving her lips a nibble.

"I'll never be fooled again." She rubbed her nose against his. "But that doesn't mean I can be with you. Us getting together doesn't feel right. You can't tell me you're all right with me having almost slept with your brother."

"No." His eyes flashed. "But, you didn't know any better. So, this one time only, I shall forgive."

"How magnanimous of you," was her dry reply. "It still changes nothing. I don't know what I want. Everything I knew has been shifted upside down. I can't even predict what will happen to me tomorrow, so you can't ask me to agree to an uncertain future."

"I told you I would get us out of here."

"For high stakes."

"Anything less wouldn't be worth it."

"If you're serious about getting us out of here, then what's your plan?"

"Can't I show rather than tell?" His words brushed warmly across her.

"Making out is not a plan."

"Maybe not to you."

She held in a smile. He was so hard to resist. His charm so arrogant, and yet it made her feel desired. However, now was not the time for them to indulge. They weren't technically alone.

"Pretend to kiss me again."

"Pretend? I don't pretend, angel." The word huffed against her lips before she felt the burning imprint of his mouth on hers.

My angel.

The words echoed in her head.

Did he say it?

He kissed her and gave her much more enthusiasm and tongue than a fake kiss needed. But then again, the more real it seemed, the better.

And it was a really good kiss.

The touch of his mouth on hers ignited her in ways she'd never imagined. It wasn't as if she'd never been kissed. The tiny spurts of excitement she felt with Samael never made her want to claw at him and draw him closer.

As Remiel deepened his embrace, she wanted to wrap herself around him. Have him inside her. Claiming her the way a man claimed his woman.

Why wait for him to claim? I should make him mine. My preciousss.

She froze. Now she sounded like Samael. Owning Remiel was not an option.

She drew away, and he made a grumble of protest.

"Get back here." His eyes opened, and they blazed, the gold in them a fiery storm.

"We have to stop."

"You started this."

"I think we've done enough for anyone watching."

"Screw the audience. What about me?" It was such a male thing to say and the grind of his body against her, the hard press of his erection against her mound so shiveringly good.

Before she could reply, Remiel rolled them, somehow managing to cover her in blankets before he sprang off her. Sue-Ellen stared at his nude buttocks as he strode away from her and rummaged through the piles of clothes.

"What's wrong?" she asked. Because she might not be very experienced, but even she knew a guy aroused as much as he was didn't just suddenly stop. "What are you doing?"

"Getting dressed."

Why? He'd seemed all too eager merely seconds ago to do things only naked people could do. Had something changed in the last minute that she didn't clue in on?

He slipped on track pants, pulling them over his tight butt. Then Remiel turned, blinding her with his excellent abs, which meant she missed the tossed items and they almost smacked her in the face. Fast reflexes stopped them.

His haste proved contagious, and she hurried to put on the garments under the cover of the blanket. Once she stopped squirming, she noted he held out his hand.

"You coming?" he asked.

"Where?" Although even if he said the edge

of the world, she might just follow.

"To the outer pit cave. Your plan worked. We've got mail."

Mail?

Curious, and worried he'd leave without her, Sue-Ellen took his hand and let him haul her to her feet. The shirt she'd borrowed hung to almost her knees, and yet she felt exposed, which was stupid. She had dressed much more indecently than this before—but that was when she remained less aware of her body and the fact that he coveted it.

"Hold my hand if you think you'll be scared," he said, wrapping his fingers around hers.

Her earlier trek through the tunnels had cured her of much of the fear, but that didn't stop her from lacing their fingers tightly.

He led them through the tunnel, keeping the fears of a collapse taking her life at bay.

They emerged into the pit area, still as dark as before except for a single pulse of light.

"What is it?" she whispered.

"Most likely a message from my brother. He's too much of a baby salamander to come see me himself."

Remiel kept his fingers laced with hers as they approached the blinking beacon. He bent over and grabbed something with his free hand.

Click. A bright beam shot out and coalesced into a shape. A familiar shape, with short hair. Almost mirror images. The facial features identical. It made her want to sing that song by Eminem about *The Real Slim Shady*. Put a few pounds on Remiel, and a person would be hard-pressed to tell the brothers apart if side-by-side.

The holographic image stared at a point to their left and overhead. "There you are, brother. Always the slow one on the uptake."

"Is he actually talking to you?" she gasped.

"Think of it as a virtual Skype call, except he can't see us."

"So he can't see me doing this?" She pointed two deadly middle fingers. It did nothing to help the situation but felt good.

"*He* can hear you, precious," 3D ghost Samael replied.

"Don't call me that. I'm not your anything."

"Are you angry I put you down the hole with my uncouth brother?"

"I'm angry I didn't shiv you."

"That's harsh." Samael grabbed at his chest. "And after all we recently meant to each other."

"What do you want?" Remiel interjected. "You don't usually call for nothing."

"I am taking Sue-Ellen back."

"No, you're not. She's mine."

"You gave her up."

"I did, and in exchange, she was to remain safe, and I was to forget."

He'd done what? Sue-Ellen listened and tried to piece it together.

"That deal is no longer in effect. As a matter of fact, in the new regime, *my* regime, I should add, you don't matter in the grand scheme of things. But I've still got a use for her." Samuel smirked.

"You don't get to have her. Even if the original deal is null and void, I lay claim to Sue-

Ellen, and while I'm at it, I'm claiming the throne."

Say what?!

Chapter Eighteen

Silence hung thickly between them for a few moments following Remiel's declaration.

How epic. Always nice when you could find the right words to inflict the maximum amount of devastation.

And Remiel would wreak a path of destruction if he had to. Because Samael had forgotten one crucial fact. He wasn't the only one with a claim to the throne.

The prophecy claimed Gold would return and lead the dragons. It didn't name which one.

I'm Gold. And Remiel was older by like five months. Not to mention, he was pure-blooded.

Technically speaking, I am king.

"You are not the one foretold. I am." The rebuttal sounded childish, and Remiel snorted.

"You are nothing but a disillusioned, spoiled brat who's been letting a power-hungry priestess lead him by his dick."

"I am the one in control."

"Not according to the handcuffs and whips." He'd rather not explain how he knew about his brother's sexual peccadillos.

"I think someone is jealous because she chose me and not you." Smugness suited Samael, but Remiel still wiped it from his face.

"Only because I turned Anastasia down first. And as to you thinking you have any say in what happens, I dare you to try. Go against one of her wishes. See what happens when you don't behave like the good little pet dragon that you are."

"I'm not a pet." The high color in his brother's face spoke of his anger—but worse, Remiel could see the embarrassment. Did Samael realize how Anastasia played him?

In the name of so-called religion, that woman had manipulated all kinds of things, wreaked tons of havoc. She was to blame for a lot of what had happened to him. When Remiel escaped—an escape counted in the ticks of seconds—he'd deal with her.

"Being a benevolent king, I won't kill you. You are, after all, my only true family, but I am hereby banning you from this continent. Begone and never show your face again." Remiel waved a hand and winked at Sue-Ellen, who gaped at him wide-eyed. Probably because his confidence awed her.

Samael did a good job of pretending to not be impressed. "Good luck with your claim on the throne. You know there's no way out of that pit."

"Didn't you pay attention to our history lessons, brother? All hoards have two entrances." A known fact. The main one for bringing in the big shit, and a small one in case subtlety is needed.

A smirk pulled his twin's lips. "Parker had that thing sealed off a while ago. Which means there is only one way out, and we both know how well that went the last time."

The last time, Remiel had been half mad with rage, not understanding where the anger and sense of loss came from. He'd climbed the walls of the pit and grabbed at the light streams caging the rim.

Not a good idea.

When he next woke, his hands were bandaged, along with his ribs, while the wrath and whatever had triggered it were gone. He'd spent a few euphoric days imagining butterflies and happy things as the incense burning non-stop from a brazier set up in the room sweetly permeated the air.

The hangover headache was totally worth it, but the munchies had seriously depleted his candy reserve.

Remiel crossed his arms and cocked his head. "Is that a challenge? I totally accept."

"You'll totally fail," hissed his sibling.

"Get your bags packed and prepare to vacate the premises, brother, because I'm getting out of here."

The hologram gave him the finger. "Like fuck you are. But if it makes you feel any better, Sue-Ellen is. Because you're right about one thing. It's time I showed Anastasia that she doesn't make all the decisions. Starting with the choice she's been forbidding me forever."

With those cryptic words, the image disappeared. Since his brother no longer flapped his gums, Remiel could hear a slight hissing sound like escaped gas. He sniffed, and his eyes widened.

Gas emerged from the hologram device, gas mixed with something else.

Magic.

Shit. "Move." The word emerged as barely a hiss as the drug, a new combination, hit Remiel hard. Hard enough that when he blinked awake, face-first in the dirt, he had a few new holes in his arm. It seemed he'd donated some blood, but that wasn't the worst of it.

Someone had taken his angel.

That was when, as Sue-Ellen would say, he lost his ever-loving shit.

Chapter Nineteen

She stood atop a mountain. A high one that elevated her above the puffy white clouds. Through the gaps in them, she could see a forest, the treetops green and lush. Through another hole, she noted the gleaming mirror sheen of tall buildings, a city but not a city of today. The flying cars gave it away.

At her back, she whirled to find a castle. It sat on several tiers of mountain, the stone block path striated with yellow pyrite—because surely no one would use gold so carelessly to make a pattern in the rock.

The castle itself was made of various elements. One wing entirely made of glass. Another the rich honey of hickory trees. Then there was the black lava rock tower, the obsidian spire rising high in the sky. *All the colors of the Septs are here.*

She somehow understood this even if she didn't know where she stood.

A trilling sound had her tilting her head to see shapes in the sky. Beautiful, sinuous shapes with massive wings.

Dragons.

I should fly with them. She stepped off the ledge, and the fist of gravity clasped her body and tugged. Wings unfurled from her back and...

Heart pounding, Sue-Ellen woke, not falling, most certainly not flying, and in the last place she would have expected.

A hotel room.

Not just any room, a lavishly appointed and seemingly expensive suite. The windows on the far wall displayed the birds-eye view of a city—but not the city of her dream. Here, the buildings were ragged and uneven, the surfaces a panoply of textures and colors. As twilight took over, color ceased to exist, and gems of light popped up to illuminate the darkness.

How did she know it was a hotel? She didn't know many houses with a sprinkler overhead, and the night table with the hotel stationery gave it away.

Where am I? How did she get here?

The last thing she recalled was...

What did she remember?

A grey void sat inside her head. How odd. She blinked and shook her head, trying to shake the cobwebs from her mind. Her memories remained out of reach. She had no beginning, no past. Maybe she'd only begun to exist in this moment.

No, I'm pretty sure I had a life. A life that was currently a blank slate.

The door to the suite opened without a knock or warning.

Sue-Ellen—her name being the one thing she knew—dragged the sheet to her chest, even though she was respectably attired in a gown. A lovely nightgown of pale gold with only thin spaghetti straps to hold it up.

A gown made for seduction—and not her style. Or was it? She didn't remember her past penchant for clothing. Demure, seductress, or something in between. She couldn't recall, but it seemed her memory was selective because she knew the man who walked in.

It's him. The boy from the dungeon. Her lips parted in a smile of greeting, and she opened her mouth to say, "Hello, Remiel," only she didn't because that wasn't Remiel.

Who's Remiel? She stumbled over her own thoughts, the name—*What name?*—sinking into the fuzzy spots of her brain.

She blinked as the man approached, and it took a moment more for her to say, "Samael?" The question quite real given the recent confusing flurry in her mind.

"Good evening, my precious."

For some reason, the term of endearment brought a shiver.

"Cold?" He reached her side and put out a hand as if to touch.

She moved away and frowned. "What am I doing here?"

"Sleeping. You'll need your rest for our honeymoon."

The words made no sense. Surely if she remembered him, she'd remember something so momentous as a wedding. "What honeymoon? We got married?" She must have gotten seriously wasted if they had because she didn't remember a damned thing.

"It was a lovely ceremony and reception. You wore your mother's dress." Lie. Mother wore jeans and got hitched in front of a judge. "We danced to our song, *Lady In Red*."

Another lie. That was her cousin Fanny's song because of the incident in the white jeans. Had to love her selective memory. *Can't remember getting hitched, but I remember telling Fanny she imagined the wet spot and I let her go to her next class.*

"Why aren't I wearing a ring?" She held up a hand.

"Because it's in my pocket for safekeeping. I made sure to book us a trip somewhere you could be yourself." It sounded so thoughtful, and his wide smile looked perfect.

She still inwardly shivered. *Because I can't trust him.*

Why not, though? This was Samael. The boy she'd pined for. She remembered him. Seeing him in that hospital bed and then the cage. Look at him now. He was no longer a prisoner.

They were together, and she was in his bed! Married. About to consummate.

Eek.

For some reason, this caused her heart to pound. She scrambled off the mattress, cheeks hot. Everything seemed so wrong.

This room. His words. Him.

He's an imposter.

There was something not right about him, starting with the hair.

It should be long, touching his shoulders in curls at the tips.

The man in front of her had it cut professional short. He also wore a suit with a tie, and his eyes glowed green with a hint of gold.

They should be pure amber.

Samael's hot gaze perused her, and she wrapped her arms around her upper body, all too aware of the thin fabric. Where was a comfortable footed onesie pajama, in flannel, when a girl needed it?

"How long have I been sleeping?"

"Long enough. Lots of long speeches at dinner. Put you right to sleep."

Just how deep would he dig the trench for his lies? "How come I can't remember anything? What happened to me?"

"Just pre-wedding jitters. You took something to calm yourself and then had a few too many glasses of champagne."

"I don't feel drunk." She'd snuck a few when Uncle was away, enough to know how it felt.

"Because you slept it off." Said a little more tersely.

"I feel so fuzzy." She held a hand to her head as if rubbing it would ease the cloud. "I need some air." And space. Space away from Samael.

For some reason, getting away seemed of prime importance.

"It's a little late for you to be wandering outside in those clothes. And there's no balcony."

"Afraid I'll throw myself off?" The words spilled from her lips, and she almost choked. Where did that come from?

"Always with the jokes. We both know you

can't fly."

Says who? The cold voice spoke only to her, and its chilly presence comforted.

She approached the window, skirting Samael, and pressed her fingers against it. Peeking out, she tried to find a landmark, something to give a sense of her location. "Where are we? What city?"

"Why all the questions? You should be happy we're finally together."

A stray thought floated to the surface. "We aren't supposed to see each other anymore. Uncle Parker was quite adamant about that."

"Parker's dead and can no longer stand in our way."

"Dead?" She didn't recall any death, and yet at the same time, the word sounded right.

Uncle's dead, but I still couldn't escape.

Escape what?

She wished her mind would stop playing games with her. It was proving quite distracting.

Samael drew close, close enough that he wrapped his arms around her from behind.

The embrace caused her to stiffen. Something about it felt wrong.

Where is the spark?

How come she never felt a spark with him?

Because he's not the man you're looking for.

Who was that talking in her head?

Me, dummy.

Her eyes widened but went unseen, given her back was pressed against his chest.

Who are you?

The chilly chuckle oddly reassured. *You. Time*

for you to wake up.

"Why so pensive?"

Too late, she realized Samael had seen her expression in the window. He turned her so that she faced him. A pinch of her chin raised her expression, and she noted, as Samael stared at her, a frown of displeasure creased his brow.

He moved his mouth close.

She leaned her head back.

"Kiss me," he demanded.

"No."

"Tease." His mouth moved toward hers, and she stared at it, slightly horrified. She pushed away from him, suddenly determined he wouldn't kiss her.

But why? She'd let him kiss her before.

Before I found out the truth.

What truth? She wanted to scream as the holes in her mind mocked her with their absence.

"What's wrong with you?" The words snapped out of him as she removed herself completely from his embrace and put some distance between them.

"You tell me what's wrong with me. There's something wrong here. You're hiding something. You did something." She pressed her hands to her temples.

Wake up.

I'm trying.

Samael's lips pressed tight. "Why do you constantly reject me? What do you see in him? We are the same. The same flesh. Face. And yet, I saw you with him. How you reacted."

"Him? Who are you talking about?"

You know who he's talking about.

Truly, Sue-Ellen wished she did because she had a feeling it would explain a lot.

"Come back here." He pointed to a spot in front of him.

She chose to move in the opposite direction along the bank of windows, wondering if she should make a run for the door leading to the hall.

He saw where she glanced. "Oh, no you don't, precious." He stalked her, a long stride with an intent green gaze hinting of gold and menace.

The door was out of reach. The windows at her back would provide no escape. They weren't the kind that opened.

"What do you want from me?"

"You. Legs spread and accepting my seed. I had hoped for willing, but I brought handcuffs in case you proved stubborn."

"Don't you dare touch me."

"I will touch you, and touch you often. How it feels is up to you. I can do gentle. *Or not.*"

The very coldness in his words took her breath. How could anyone be so...evil? "Why are you doing this?"

At the query, he shrugged. "Because I can. Because I'm king. Because getting inside you first and planting my seed will hurt him more than anything else I can do."

"Him who?" Who did Samael keep referring to? The answer hinted just out of reach.

"Don't play stupid. We both know you prefer my brother, and yet it was I who tried so hard. I was so patient, too. But the process took so long. The treatment drugs could only be applied slowly."

What drugs?

"And then, when that was done, they didn't want me to waste my essence, not with it in such high demand with the Septs. I had to wait some more while they started you on hormone treatments to stimulate your eggs."

"What treatments?" And why did she want to pinch herself awake? Surely, this was a nightmare.

"You are now ready for me. Ready to be the vessel for the gift I will bestow upon you."

"You can keep your gift."

"It's answers like that which got you into trouble in the first place. I would have thought your last lesson would have taught you some respect."

"You threw me into a pit." The memory hit her suddenly.

"I did, and I'd do it again to punish you. I put you with my cave-dwelling brother to teach you a lesson. To show you how much better off you are with me."

Samael had a brother? The truth uncoiled slowly in her head. "Remiel lives in the cave." Remiel was the boy she'd fallen for. The man who'd given up his life for her. The dragon who claimed she was his hoard.

And Samael had just stolen her.

She shook her head. "Oh, Samael. What have you done?"

"I did nothing wrong," he shouted. Green

fire danced in his eyes, the gold a mere pinprick in the center. "I courted you, and respected you, yet still you prefer him over me. Always him." He screamed at her now, the warm spittle like drops of acid spraying.

He acted like a child, one who'd had his toy taken away from him. One who could not handle his jealousy.

I don't really care. He didn't have the right to treat her like this. He didn't have the right to threaten or hurt or do anything to her.

No one would ever have that kind of control over her again.

Ignoring his angry countenance, she turned away from him and noted through the glass just how high they were. High enough for a dragon to fly.

"Does Anastasia know you've brought me here?" she asked as she watched a shadow skimming over rooftops. She had a theory. An outrageous theory.

"Of course she knows. Who do you think helped me install you here?"

The pieces fell into place, and Sue-Ellen wanted to shake Samael. Shake him for being so clueless. "She put me here. She knows what you're planning to do to me." That added only more credence to her theory. For some reason, she felt prompted to warn him. "Samael, you have to leave. Now. It's a trap."

"What are you talking about?"

"You're being used. The priestess is about to betray you."

"Betray me? She wouldn't dare. I am the Golden king she's been waiting for." The arrogance refused to see the truth.

"Are you the one foretold?"

"It's been declared. I am the Gold returned."

"But you're not pure Gold." A few more pieces of the puzzle clicked.

"Close enough."

"Is it?" Because Remiel was a pure Golden dragon while Samael was not. Given Anastasia was all about the prophecy and the return of the true king, that meant Samael was the dupe.

"I am—" Samael never got to finish his statement.

As the door once again opened without warning, Anastasia sauntered in. Still looking like a bitch. Still in need of a slap.

Her rouged lips curved into a smirk. "There's the Golden mutt."

His attention veered from Sue-Ellen to the priestess. "What did you call me?"

"You're a mutt, dear child. A mixed-blood." Anastasia walked into the room, the height of arrogance. Head held high. Smirk quite distinct.

"I am Golden."

"Half Golden, which makes you useful."

"More than useful. I am your king. You will show me respect."

A loud derisive snort left the priestess. "You are not the king. The true king is coming. Remiel has declared himself."

"And? He does it too late. I"—Samael stabbed himself in the chest with a finger—"have already declared myself. His statement changes nothing."

"On the contrary, it changes everything. It seems he's finally learned from his time in the cage. I knew one day, with the right incentive, I'd get him to break out."

As the priestess argued with Samael, Sue-Ellen felt her mental thoughts slowly coming back to her. Memories tumbled into place, and she added to them as she listened to Anastasia and Samael quarrel.

"Remiel is a loose cannon. You said so yourself."

"So are you, apparently. I thought I said the girl was off-limits."

Samael's shoulders stiffened, and a thickness entered his tone. "The girl is mine."

"No, the girl is your brother's. The fact that you keep trying to trick her hasn't changed her feelings for him. She prefers the real Golden king over you."

The words made Sue-Ellen wince. They were cruel. So cruel.

"Well, he apparently didn't feel the same way, given he never turned away those women you paraded in front of him."

The what?

"Only once he made the deal to forget. He proved a lot more amenable to attempts to breed once the girl was gone."

"That deal is over. He remembers everything now. But it won't do him any good. He's stuck in the pit, and I'm here with Sue-Ellen. So if I were you, I'd shut up now before I shut your mouth permanently."

"Threats? Do you think that's wise?" Anastasia's lips curled into a cruel sneer.

"It's not a threat, it's a promise."

"Still acting like a boy rather than a man."

"This *boy* is going to claim this woman, and there's nothing you can do to stop me. And you can tell my brother that."

"I already did." Anastasia smirked. "Would you like to hear his reply?"

Sue-Ellen kind of did. However, she had something more pressing to state. "There is not going to be any claiming by anyone. Not you. Not Remiel. Not anybody. I'm done playing your games."

"The girl finally finds her tongue. Not that I care. You were simply the bait."

Bait for which fish? She was so tired of it all, and she placed most of the blame on the priestess in front of her. "Why hasn't anybody killed you yet? Surely not everyone's aim is that bad?"

"Smart words for a girl who was caught so easily. You never even knew there were two."

Way to play on her guilt. "You won't fool me again. I'm done with all this." She pushed away from the window, only to halt immediately as both the priestess and Samael stiffened.

"You'll be done when I say you're done," Samael snarled.

"You can't tell me what to do. I've had enough of that." Sue-Ellen rammed her elbow back, knowing it would hurt—*crack*, oh boy did it hurt—

but the glass-plated window webbed, and a second blow shoved the weakened shards outward. As they fell to the ground in a glinting glass shower, she dove out, evading the grasping fingers of Samael and his shouted, "Don't you dare!"

Oh, she dared, all right.

The wind fluttered past her cheeks, and she closed her eyes, enjoying the sensation of freedom. But the sidewalk fast approached.

Come out, come out, wherever you are.

She sang to her inner beast, knowing she was in there.

About time you called for me. Grumbled even as her primal self burst free and flapped her wings for the first time.

Holy shit, look at me. I'm flying.

Only, it turned out flying wasn't as easy as it looked. Just flapping wasn't enough. While slower than before, she continued to plummet!

Chapter Twenty

He no sooner lost his mind at her disappearance than Remiel tried to climb the shaft. Halfway up, snarling and roaring with rage—letting them know he came to eat them—a piece of paper fluttered down.

For some reason, he caught it. Read it. The words on the note burned in his brain.

Samael has your hoard. It included an address. Easy to memorize. As for the hint? *Look for a river.* It proved to be his ticket out of the cave network without bloodshed. But he'd be back. He had some scores to settle.

With rage driving his actions, much of what happened during his escape proved a blur. Remiel had only one focus. Finding his angel.

And taking care of Samael once and for all.

When he emerged into freedom, he took a deep breath and uttered a challenge to the sky. The world. To any and all listening.

The king has returned.

He didn't get a reply.

The mighty flapping of his wings pulled him through the sky, and he coasted along the air currents, letting them propel him along. He knew his geography, knew so many things, the facts he'd memorized once useless… No more.

He moved quickly. Swiftly. Unseen.

Deadly.

He couldn't delay. Not while his brother had his angel. If he or that red witch harmed a single hair on her head…the world would burn.

His destination proved closer than he could have hoped for. The tall tower housing the luxury hotel appeared as a lit beacon in the night sky. But he only had eyes for one floor. The top floor. A top floor with a bank of windows, one with a hole in it.

A face peered through the broken pane, a face he saw in the mirror every day.

There you are, brother.

Samael didn't see him. Remiel, on the other hand, saw Anastasia move behind his brother and lift her head to toss him a wink before shoving Samael out the opening.

Ha. Served him right.

Remiel ignored his falling brother to trumpet a challenge. If it could have been translated, it would have sounded something like, *For the crime of taking my hoard from me, I mark thee for death.*

The priestess heard him and lifted her head. She smirked and mouthed something. "What hoard? You're too late. The woman is gone."

Gone? That quickly, his gaze veered downward, and he noted the cluster of people on the ground, grouped around something. Something on the sidewalk.

He arrowed toward them, his mighty shape casting a pall that even the night sky couldn't mask.

The humans scattered before his mightiness.

Some of them bleating. One pissing himself. He'd seen sheep with more decorum. They left behind their object of curiosity.

A scrap of fabric. Gold. Silken. The scent so clearly that of his angel.

But no angel wearing it.

There was also no blood and no guts, which he took as a good sign. But he did have a problem.

Where had she gone? Craning his head left and right, seeking with all his senses, didn't give him a scent to trace. But he did feel a tug that a—

"Did you know ssshe has wings now?" lisped Samael, interrupting his concentration. Wearing only pants and no shirt to accommodate his massive wings, his brother stood blocking his view with his hybrid shape.

You. Remiel might have thought the word, but his sibling heard and his gaze narrowed.

"Get out of my head."

You took Sue-Ellen.

"I did, and she liked it."

Liar.

He blew at his brother, a hot golden mist that pushed his sibling back on his heels but didn't dissolve his skin as hoped.

"No lies. I took your woman and made her mine. And I'll take her again as soon as—"

Pop. Pop. Pop. The crack of gunfire peppered the air, most of the shots going astray and digging into the sidewalk, sending cement chips flying. Blood splattered when a bullet tore through Samael's wing.

Before the same could happen to Remiel, he

took a moment to pull his scales hard, tightening them into a bulletproof shield. It would repel most missiles. However, it took effort to hold, especially against unknown numbers. There was more than one gun firing. They'd been ambushed.

A dragon knew when to fight and when to fly so he could regroup and return to win the day.

With a mighty pounce, Remiel took to the sky, losing track of Samael—as if he cared what happened to his errant sibling.

His mighty wings pulled, grabbing the very air itself and molding it for his use, bringing him aloft, high enough the bullets couldn't reach him. Only then did he loosen his scales.

He took stock of the situation below. The occasional cracks let him count the various opponents. Five. At opposite ends firing. Someone had planned this. Someone who knew he, or Samael, would be there.

A setup. But who orchestrated it? Who dared to try and kill the Golden king?

I should find out.

And kill them.

A shape shimmered into existence beside him, a gold and green hybrid and, dangling from his clawed hands, a human with wide eyes.

What are you doing? he trilled the question.

Samael shook his prize. "Asssking thisss human why he was shooting at usss."

"The monsters must die!" the human gleefully yelled, suddenly coming to life. He flailed his hands at Samael's face while swinging his legs to push off his abdomen. A strange foam erupted from his mouth, and the body quivered.

Samael loosened his grip, and the human fell. Fell to the ground below with a final thump. Samael then looked at Remiel. "Looks like the pitchforks are coming out."

Probably the only true and smart thing Samael had ever said. If the humans firing weren't some kind of fluke group, then it might be the start of something bigger—and more violent.

Excellent. *War is coming.* What part would he play?

There was only one role suited for him. He just needed to ensure that no one tried to take it. As Remiel flapped his wings alongside his brother, he debated the merits of tearing his head off now and saving himself the trouble later.

Death was so final, though. Kill Samael, and he'd lose the joy of torturing not only his mortal enemy but also his only sibling.

A teeny tiny part of him didn't want to kill the only true relative he had.

Before he could fully decide what to do with his brother, the *whup-whup-whup* of 'copter blades cut through the whistling wind.

"That can't be good. Another time, brother." With a salute, Samael departed, and since Remiel had better things to do than play with mechanical toys, he took flight in a different direction.

Leaving behind the sound of helicopters, he returned to his original dilemma. Where was Sue-Ellen? How should he decide which way to go? The world was a very strange place. Also a big place for a dragon used to a tiny sphere of his own.

Feel for her.

Wasn't most of his problem the fact that he felt too much?

Use that to find her.

How? he asked, and yet, at the same time, he took a peek within, searched for that tiny tendril, the one that had linked him to his angel since the first time they touched.

There it was, a weak pulse in… He banked and captured a new air current in a slightly altered direction. He wound that tiny tendril around a fist and pulled himself toward it. Closer. Closer.

It abruptly disappeared, and for a moment, he froze in the air and coasted.

What did it mean? Was she dead? No. Not dead. He refused to believe it. He'd know if she'd died. No hole suddenly gaped in his heart. She lived but was hidden from him.

Not too many people could do that—but dragons could. He banked his wings and studied the lay of the land below. The evening sky meant only the barest shadow ghosted on the ground to betray his passage.

He needed to think. Where would Sue-Ellen go now that she'd escaped? Where would she feel safe?

There was only one place he'd wager. Her brother.

If Remiel remembered his politics class at all, taught by Anastasia and a ruler—lined sharply as a blade—then Brandon, the false Gold, had married a Silvergrace girl. But how to contact them?

This was where his knowledge and memory came in handy. Anastasia had spent as much time teaching Remiel as she did having him studied. As a result, he knew all the family names. Their domains. He could have traced on a map the places considered held by certain Septs. She'd trained him and Samael to one day be king. Funny how they'd forgotten to question how they could both rule when the prophecy called for only one.

Knowing what Remiel did meant he knew where to go in every major city to get some information. First, however, he needed pants.

Remiel outfitted himself before he paid a visit to the Silvergrace offices the following day. Although *offices* was a misnomer, given it acted more like an embassy to the Silvers in this neutral zone.

A few major cities around the world were ruled by other cryptozoid sects. Here in Las Vegas, the Djinn had a strong foothold but loved to do business with dragons. No surprise, the Silver Sept owned a sprawling silver-hued hotel and casino resort. Someone in their expansive offices would have the information Remiel needed.

Despite a lack of Americanized identification, Remiel strolled right in and didn't worry about making an appointment.

People would bow to his will and thank him for taking time out of his busy day to visit. They couldn't move fast enough once they realized who they dealt with. It took only a flash of his eyes, a golden flare, to have people scurrying to do his bidding.

In no time at all, he was ushered to the top

floor and placed in the presence of an older woman. Dressed bohemian style, she sat in the corner of a large and lavish room. A room with no windows and only one door. A steel door for a fancy prison?

Not again.

When the young female who escorted him would have shut them in, Remiel stopped the door from closing. "This stays open."

"But the soundproofing—"

The older woman held up a hand. "It's all right, Babette. I think the boy needs reassurance he won't come to any harm."

"You think I fear you?" He almost snorted in disbelief.

"What should I think? You won't allow us to be alone in a room together. Or are you going to claim you're keeping the door open that we might preserve my virtue because, I can assure you, that ship sailed a long time ago."

He wouldn't be bested by this woman.

Instead of replying, he slammed the door shut. He then took a seat and stared.

Stared for a while.

Stared until the woman frowned. "You aren't Samael D'Ore."

He shook his head and smiled.

"Another Gold dragon. I'll be damned," the woman murmured.

"Shouldn't you be curtsying instead?"

At that, her lips twitched. "Such arrogance. What is your name?"

"My title is your highness, but my birth name as inscribed on my shell is Remiel D'Ore. I am the last Golden king."

A king who got no respect, as the old woman giggled. "This is getting to be absolutely entertaining. And here I am being rude not introducing myself. I am Waida Silvergrace Montague. Sister to—"

"The matriarch of the Silver Sept. Yes, I know. I had my share of history lessons, and I don't really care right now about your lineage. I am here for another reason. I'm looking for someone. A girl."

"Sue-Ellen Mercer."

He bolted from his seat and, in a blink of an eye, stood in front of the gray-haired woman, hands braced on the armrest of her chair, looming. "You know her. Where is she?"

"According to the phone call I got a few hours ago, she's safe."

"Safe where? What have you done with Sue-Ellen?" His fingers gripped the armrests tight and shook the chair a bit.

Waida arched a brow. "I've done nothing. No one is stupid enough to harm Brandon's sister."

"I want her brought to me."

"I can't do that."

Can't? What an ugly word. Also an utterly unacceptable one. "She's mine."

The older woman's gaze narrowed. "Actually, given she's unmated and fatherless, it falls on her brother to protect her."

"Tell him I need her back. Sue-Ellen is mine." *All mine.* His only treasure.

"Someone seems a touch possessive. Seems

to me like the girl should be allowed to make that decision."

"You're right, she should." Because he had no doubt she'd make the right choice. "Let me know where she is, and I will speak to her at once."

"Aren't you a demanding one? In many ways like your brother, and yet not."

Nothing like him. Nothing… "You've dealt with Samael? What do you know of him?"

"Not as much as I'd like. Just that he paid our house a visit a while back. I thought him cocky and arrogant, but I see he was but a pale imitation of the real thing."

"My brother had a spoiled childhood."

"And what was yours like?"

"I am not going to divulge some sob-worthy tale of how I was stuck in a cage most of my life. Adversity makes me stronger, and as you can see, the cage couldn't hold me."

"Who held you captive? Parker?"

"Eventually, but I was first a prisoner to the Crimson priestess. She is the one who oversaw my upbringing, and when I wouldn't bow to the red priestess's heel, I was locked away."

Waida's lips pursed. "That woman is becoming a real problem."

"Becoming? I'd say she's well past that point." But fear not, he had plans for her—he just needed to grab a few ingredients first and find the right kind of tree for burning.

"Hate her if you like, it doesn't matter. She has put certain things in motion, and we now have no choice but to follow. A pity we didn't know about you before. She's already presented Samael as the Golden heir."

"A false heir. I am the true Gold."

"Are you? I can't believe we've found yet another one." Waida shook her head. "It's interesting how a year ago we had no Goldens to unite the Septs, and now we have too many."

"I am the only true Gold."

"But are you the one foretold?" She leaned forward and fixed him with an intent gaze. "Do you have what it takes, Remiel D'Ore, to lead your people past the dark times coming? Your brother, Samael, with the help of the Crimson Sept, has amassed a large force. The Reds, Blues, and some of the Greens have thrown in their allegiance to him."

"They will change their minds once they realize he is the imposter."

"Will they? He's promising them the world. What can you give them? By your own admission, you were a prisoner, which means you don't even have treasure to buy an army."

"Buy?" He arched a brow. "A king does not buy troops. They serve. And I do have a treasure. It's just been misplaced, hence why I'm here."

Waida quickly understood. "You're speaking of the girl, aren't you?"

"Yes. Where is she? Take me to her at once."

"I can tell you, but you won't be able to take her. Especially if her brother gets there first."

"I've already told you this brother has no claim."

"And I told you it would be her choice."

"You disobey your king!" Once again, he loomed over the seated woman. "Tell me now." The timbre of the demand reverberated in the room, filled with power.

The older woman licked her lips and shook her head. "Oh, you're good. Strong, too. Almost strong enough to make me obey, but you're also unschooled."

"I could kill you with a twist of my wrist," he growled, grabbing her by the throat and lifting her. He knew he was being irrational, but at the moment, all he could think of was this woman thought to stand between him and his treasure.

She is keeping me from my angel.

"Don't make threats you won't follow through with. First rule of kingship."

"I don't make idle threats."

Snort. The old woman still had no respect. "You won't kill me because kings don't kill their subjects. And they most certainly don't murder their advisors."

"You're not my advisor. I work alone."

"Not anymore. A good thing you found me because if you're going to rule, you can't just rush in head first and command people."

"I am king."

"Yes, and if you want people to listen and respect you, you have to more than just announce it. We'll talk more of that later."

"You really think you're going to advise me." The idea seemed ludicrous, and yet the old woman seemed quite serious.

"A king can't rule alone."

"Which is why I need the girl."

"If I tell you where she is, will you promise to listen?"

"Give me Sue-Ellen."

"I can't give her to you, only she can make that choice, but how about if you listen, I won't just help you find your queen, I'll show you how to give her the world."

"Very well. I agree to your terms." Because even Sue-Ellen would have to admit the world was a pretty damned good gift.

Which was how he found himself on a private jet that same night and then driven the next morning to a large compound behind several layers of security.

Dressed in a suit, he brought his confidence with him to win over Sue-Ellen.

What he should have brought instead was dragoness repellent.

Chapter Twenty-one

The distant commotion drew Sue-Ellen. Who could ignore the excited chitter of women and occasional thumps as jostling occurred for a better position?

What had them so excited?

Then again, did it take much? Sue-Ellen's arrival at the Silvergrace manor—and by manor she meant holy square footage, practically a small town—certainly caused consternation. Sue-Ellen wanted to sink into a puddle of mud when she'd arrived dressed in a very pink tracksuit courtesy of the silver-haired girl who had literally grabbed her out of the sky when Sue-Ellen jumped out of the building. The encounter was…interesting.

The timing proved fortuitous, however. The other girl, a few years older than Sue-Ellen, had switched from her dragon to human shape as soon as they alit on a roof. "If you're going to fly, you might want to try flapping your wings."

"I wasss flapping them," Sue-Ellen grumbled with a lisp. They were obviously defective.

"Remind me to show you the proper way to fly. And whatever you do, don't let Aunt Yvonne know you can't. She's old school, which means she'll take you to the top of the highest building she knows and shove you off."

"Your aunt sounds nuts."

"She is. I hope to be just like her someday," sighed the girl with obvious hero worship.

"Who are you?" Sue-Ellen asked.

"Deka Silvergrace at your service. And just in time, too. Good thing Auntie told me to rush."

"Someone told you to come find me?"

"Actually, her exact words were 'don't let the stupid girl meat pie herself on the sidewalk.'"

"But how did your aunt know I would be falling?"

"She just did, and we don't ask questions."

Sue-Ellen could respect that. She had a few relatives that demanded the same kind of unwavering respect.

"Here, you can wear this until we get to the car." This being a long trench coat the woman tossed her way. Sue-Ellen flipped shapes and quickly slipped on the jacket. While she accepted the gift, she didn't plan to stick with Deka. It would put the girl in too much danger. She highly doubted Samael and Anastasia would let her go so easily.

Tying the sash over her nakedness, Sue-Ellen looked up to see Deka staring.

With eyes wide, she jabbed a finger in Sue-Ellen's direction. "Holy jumping jeepers. I know you."

"I doubt it." Sue-Ellen knew very few people.

"Actually, I do since I and the other girls went looking for you a little while back. You're

Brandon's sister. We gave up trying to rescue you after your birthday party when you blew him off."

This strange rescuer knew who Sue-Ellen was, which meant, "You know my brother?"

"Know him? He's married to my cousin. Although he totally could have been mine if I'd found him first. But even if he married the wrong girl, we're still family. Just don't think you can borrow the car," Deka said, pointing to the silver Mercedes parked on the street with the dark-tinted windows. "That baby is mine."

That baby took corners much too fast.

It was rather exhilarating. Sue-Ellen rather coveted the feeling and eyed the car with new interest.

The chance encounter with Deka was how Sue-Ellen had ended up on a plane, wearing a hot pink tracksuit on her way to the stronghold of the Silver Sept.

Arriving at the manor, she'd endured an eerie *Village of the Damned* moment. Females, all sporting shades of silver hair, some with hints of red, blue, even green, poured out of everywhere it seemed. From the archway off the main entrance, crowding the balcony for the staircase. So many curious eyes, many of them glowing green. It almost froze her.

Danger.

She didn't need the warning to flare her nostrils at the threat of so many predators in one place.

It didn't help that a little silver imp ran from between a pair of legs and skidded to a stop in front of her. A nose covered in freckles wrinkled. "She smells funny."

Sue-Ellen, having been raised amongst cousins in the swamp, knew what to do in this kind of situation. She bent down low and whispered. "Careful, little girl. I've eaten squirrels bigger than you. And I'm hungry."

Eyes rounded—with delight—lips curved in a lovely horrified O—of pleasure—and the little predator-in-training ran off squealing—and giggling.

First test passed. Several of the bodies studying her disappeared, leaving her alone with only a handful.

One of them, a stately woman dressed in a pantsuit with her hair pinned up, eyed her with interest. "Another Mercer in an unascended state. I see Parker experimented on more than just one family member."

"Even after his death, Parker is still managing to throw us surprises," said another woman that Sue-Ellen actually recognized. Zahra, the matriarch of the Silvergrace clan, rumored to be the most powerful female dragon. A claim that Anastasia scoffed at.

"My uncle had a lot of secrets."

"And how many do you have, girl?" Zahra fixed an intent stare on her, stripping away any lies and camouflage she might have had.

"Secrets are what kept me as a peon under my uncle's thumb. I'm tired of being used."

"Then stop." Deka, who'd stuck around, hopped off the credenza she'd perched herself on—a piece of furniture straight out of some hoity-toity magazine done in distressed white and silver gilt. "Since rolling over and playing nice hasn't worked for you, why keep doing it?"

"I thought I was protecting someone," she grumbled, and even now, Sue-Ellen wondered if she should go back. Put herself back in harm's way just to save an arrogant dragon.

"Who were you protecting?" asked the woman in the bun. "Another Mercer family member? I don't recall Brandon mentioning anyone else being taken."

"Not exactly family."

"I bet I know why she didn't run." Deka jabbed a finger in her direction. "You stuck with your uncle for a boy!"

No point in lying. "Actually, he's a man now and utterly arrogant on account of who he is. Although, you'd think he'd know better than to be so cocky, given he's prisoner in some pit."

"Who are you talking about?" Yolanda asked. "I wasn't aware that any more of our kind were being kept prisoner."

Given all the curious expressions, there was no point in hiding the truth. Besides, secrets were what led to all the troubles. "I guess you guys haven't heard about Remiel yet. He's Samael's brother. Half-brother. And he's a pure Gold."

After that announcement, she spent a good two hours answering questions. Only once the matriarch and her second—the steely-eyed Yolanda—felt she'd siphoned her brain dry did they let Sue-Ellen escape—to a guest room.

She wasn't a prisoner, but neither was Sue-Ellen in the mood to brave the big, wide world. Let her enjoy the safety promised within these walls. She deserved it, dammit.

Taking the time to shower and dress, she wondered what the Silvergrace Sept would do about Remiel. Sue-Ellen had explained his captive status. How they'd used Sue-Ellen against him. She'd asked if they would rescue and was told to not, "worry about it." They wouldn't give her the slightest inkling as to what they planned to do with the knowledge.

Exiting the bathroom, a new and clean woman, Sue-Ellen wasn't surprised to find Deka lying across her bed. The silver-haired girl pointed a remote at the television screen. "Is this the guy you were lusting after?"

Glancing at the screen, Sue-Ellen immediately noted the long golden hair left loose across his shoulders. The white shirt tucked into snug jeans. "That's him. Remiel. But how?" Had Samael finally let him go? She could see his lips moving on the screen. "What's he saying?" Sue-Ellen asked, drawing close enough to flop on the bed.

Deka raised the volume. "Basically, 'hey dudes, ignore my brother. I'm the real dragon king.'"

"That's it?"

"Isn't that enough? I mean, he just announced that the Goldens are back and there's going to be some trouble."

Sue-Ellen frowned. "He didn't really say

that, did he?"

"No, but the implication is totally there. It was incredibly hot the way he just kind of boldly stated it. I thought that Samael dude was cute, but this guy… He's just oozing sexy, and my birthday is like weeks away. So I'm in dire need of a mate. Any pointers on how to attract him?"

"You want to date Remiel?" The shocked query burst from her lips.

"Date. Fuck. Keep. Can you imagine the brownie points I'd get if I snared myself the Golden king as a mate? Not to mention, the man has gotta be a beast in bed."

"You. Will. Not. Touch. Him." Without taking a breath or even a blink, Sue-Ellen found herself flipping Deka onto the bed, her arm over the back of her head, her knee shoved into the middle of her spine. She hissed, "He's mine."

Appalled at her behavior, Sue-Ellen almost apologized, but Deka shrugged and uttered, "Fair enough. But since you call dibs on him, keep me in mind for his brother."

"Samael is a psychopath who threw me in a pit."

"A man with a bit of backbone. Love it."

"You're nuts."

"Thanks. Don't worry. Soon, you'll understand how the world works."

"What's that supposed to mean?" Sue-Ellen asked.

"Just that the world revolves around our kind."

"I'm not your kind."

"What are you talking about? I saw you. You're dragon."

"No, I'm not," a vehement rebuttal, and yet, didn't she hear a cold chuckle? *Fool. You won't be able to ignore it for much longer.*

"Yeah, you are. Don't forget. I not only saw you in your unascended shape, I can smell it on you, and it's getting stronger."

Great. Building body odor. Just what every girl wanted. "If I'm anything because of Uncle's experiments, it's a wyvern, not a dragon. You're mistaken."

"No mistake. I thought you knew."

Could it be true? Sure, it had happened to Brandon. He'd become a dragon. But surely it hadn't worked twice?

The phone on the nightstand—an ornate pewter-colored thing with a rotary dial and a proper headset—rang.

Dring-a-ling.

"You going to answer that?" Deka asked from underneath her.

Rolling off the woman, Sue-Ellen grabbed for the phone.

"Hello?" said tentatively.

"Are you all right?" Her brother's voice boomed in her ear.

She grimaced. "Not anymore. I think I'm deaf." It might have been a while since they'd spoken—*my fault*—but she'd still recognize his voice anywhere. It brought a prickle to her eyes.

"Don't be a smartass with me. What's this I hear about you taking a dive out of a building? I don't care if you've decided you don't want to talk to me, but I won't have you hurting yourself." Because he loved her.

She knew that, and the tears slipped free. "I wasn't trying to kill myself."

"Then why would you do something so stupid and crazy?"

"I have wings, Brandon."

Those soft words abruptly silenced him. She couldn't even hear him breathing.

"Brandon?"

A heavy sigh filled her ear. Then a stream of profanity that would have probably made her prudish uncle—who actually became a priest—die a second time had he heard it. The man had a fit every time the Mercers cussed, swore, and bragged about premarital sex.

"I'm so sorry, baby sis. I should have better protected you from our uncle."

"It wasn't your fault. You didn't know."

"I did know. He did the same thing to me. Which is why I don't understand why you didn't come with me when I came to rescue you."

How to explain that she'd stayed and put herself in danger because she thought she loved a boy.

Thought?

If Sue-Ellen was honest, wouldn't she admit she *still* loved him? Remiel hadn't changed. He was still a victim of her uncle. Still the boy who'd given her electric shivers every time they touched. But was that reason enough for them to stay together?

"It's complicated," was what she finally told

her brother. "It still is complicated, which is why I can't stay here, Brandon. I might be putting these people in danger. It's very possible Samael or Anastasia will want me back." Especially if Sue-Ellen truly was becoming a dragon.

"They can try, but they are not getting you back. I can promise you that. So sit tight. Don't you dare set foot outside that mansion until I am back in the country."

"Where are you?"

"In the Caribbean on a honeymoon with my wife."

Wife? Sue-Ellen could have cried. *So many things I missed.*

That would stop now. She was no longer under Uncle Theo's or Anastasia's thumb.

Deka leaned over and hollered, "Don't worry Brand, we've got your sister covered. She ain't going nowhere. Even better, she's gonna hook me up with an evil dragon overlord." The scary part of that claim? Deka was entirely serious.

Crazy woman.

Almost as crazy as the man entering the mansion. She returned to the moment and the commotion on the first floor. All the residents of the house seemed to be drawn to the vestibule, a sea of silver with glints of color. But only one crown was covered in gold.

"Remiel!" She merely whispered his name, but somehow, he heard. His head lifted, and his amber gaze found her. His nostrils flared, and his eyes filled with golden fire.

"Angel."

The word echoed inside her head. The possessive, low tone squeezed her. It was both exhilarating and frightening. She took a step back and shook her head, trying to dislodge the resonating feeling in her that urged her to fly and meet him.

Why am I holding back? He's there. He's mine. The vehemence of the statement had her taking a step back.

"Oh no, you don't."

She could hear him talking to her even if no one else seemed to notice. This was between them alone.

Another step and she couldn't see him anymore until Remiel took a pace toward her, but further progress found itself impeded as too many women stood in his way. Young women.

Want to bet they're unmarried? The sly retort had her flexing the fingers hanging down by her sides.

Hands off. She wanted to scream it out loud as she swooped on him, prepared to make a bold claim.

No claiming. Was she insane?

Well, she had hung around Deka. But surely craziness couldn't be caught that quickly and easily? After how she'd gotten burned by the D'Ore brothers, she needed to stay away.

Making any claim on Remiel would end badly—for her.

Besides, the same reasons that kept her and Samael apart still existed, even more so where Remiel was concerned.

A gator with the true Golden king? It could never happen.

She tucked her hands behind her back and moved until her back pressed against the door to her room, but she didn't enter it. She stood and listened.

A few murmurs down below almost proved her undoing.

"He's mine. I saw him first."

"You did not see him first because you weren't even here when he walked in."

The women fought over him, but he belonged to Sue-Ellen.

"I'm gonna lick him."

Not without a tongue, the hussy wouldn't.

"I am totally going to claim him!"

"You can't claim him. He's the king. Only he can claim a queen, and by queen, I mean me."

They were both wrong because Remiel belonged to Sue-Ellen. *Mine.*

And I shall hug him and...

She shook her head as the fierce need to possess took her.

What is wrong with me?

Remiel was most certainly not hers, and why would she want to own him?

Because if he's mine, they can't have him. It wouldn't take long before Remiel found himself bound to a dragoness. The last true Golden dragon. Sue-Ellen could see how whom he chose would prove important to the future of his kind.

It wasn't as if he'd suffer from the interest in him by beautiful women. He could take his pick of shape and size. He could choose to build his empire by aligning with an old family, one already rich and powerful and able to cement his claim.

All things Sue-Ellen couldn't give him, and despite what Deka said, she knew she couldn't be a dragon. She didn't have that kind of luck.

But the silver lining is I am still alive. And alone.

Never alone. The words whispered. Whose words, though?

Whirling, she grabbed the knob to the door at her back and turned it, but she wasn't fast enough to miss his bellow.

"Enough!" The command, all male, and very powerful, reverberated in the hall. Immediate silence reigned.

For a few seconds.

Then giggles.

"Look at him trying to give orders."

"We'll have to cure him of that habit."

"Silly man."

Fools. They might laugh now, but Remiel was just coming into his strength. Surely they could feel the rawness of it. It pulsed within him and would grow. He would have to grow in power if he truly wanted to be king.

History will tell stories of him.

She was about to step into the room when she heard, in her head, a very distinctly growled, *"Don't go anywhere. I'm coming."*

What? Whirling around, she stepped closer to the rail in time to catch a blurring glimpse of gold. Then nothing.

One moment, Remiel stood there. The next?

Poof. Gone. Vanished into thin air, causing consternation.

Everyone peeked over their shoulders and spun around. But Remiel had well and truly vanished.

"Where did he go?" The awe in their tones served only to reinforce her belief.

Do I want to be with a guy whose every move is being scrutinized?

"Of course you do." The soft words came out of nowhere and should have startled her.

But she knew that voice.

Opening her mouth, she managed only a tiny squeak before his hand over her mouth stopped further noise.

"You must contain your excitement at seeing me."

The worse part about his arrogance? He wasn't entirely wrong. A part of her truly was exhilarated at his appearance.

Hand over her mouth, and his whole body pressed against her, invisibly, she might add, which made it freaky, Remiel frog-walked her back into her room. The door shut with a click. Only then did he let her go.

She whirled around and saw nothing. She began to thrust with her fist, jabbing the air in front of her, trying to find him.

"You have a strange way of saying hi," he claimed, shimmering into sight. He looked so pleased with himself.

"This is for trying to make me pee my pants," she snapped before she slugged him in the gut. She might as well have punched a wall. The throb in her knuckles and his wider smirk only served to make her scowl. Mostly because he was so damned cute.

"I missed you, too."

"Did not. Why are you here?"

"Because I had to find you."

Name a woman who could resist a man saying that. Who could possibly stand firm against him when he said that to her with such sincerity? "I hate you." She threw herself at him and mashed her lips against his.

His mouth didn't seem to mind the attack. His hands reached around to firmly cup her ass in his hands. He yanked her closer to him, taking over control of the fervent embrace.

"I knew you missed me," he said, much too pleased with himself, between kisses.

"I thought you were dead." Knowing he wasn't, knowing he'd come looking for her, was the most euphoric feeling in the world.

Although, if these kisses continued, she might revise that last statement.

"I'm not that easy to kill." His teeth pulled at her lower lip. Teasing it while his hands roamed the shape of her ass, weighing and kneading the globes, grinding her against his evident arousal.

It was a little too much, too quickly. Her head and heart felt so muddled. She pulled back. "How did you find me?" Her lips throbbed, and she stared at his mouth. Wanted his mouth, his kisses a drug that made her limbs weak and her eyelids heavy. "Did Anastasia let you out?"

"Not exactly. I escaped."

"I thought that pit we were in was foolproof?"

Remiel nipped her lower lip and then sucked it. "To an ordinary dragon, perhaps. But I am special." And then he proceeded to explain just how simple it was.

She gaped at him and might have shuddered a few times as he nonchalantly talked about wading through a nest of very angry arachnids—they were quite peeved he'd killed their cousins. Then he went on to wrestle several dozen serpents into submission—the knots would take a long time to unravel according to his boasting. He'd finished his escape with a long swim on a single breath via an icy cold underground stream that shot out eventually into the bottom of a large lake.

"You really did escape, so why are you here?"

"To find you. I'll always find you."

"I almost wasn't here to find. I jumped out of a window and almost kissed pavement."

"So I heard. I missed your dive out the window by a moment."

"But how did you know to go there?" She didn't even know where she was until Deka told her.

"I found you because we're connected."

Her brow furrowed. "Connected how?"

"You do realize how cute it is when you frown, right?"

"Don't change the subject."

"Why not? You haven't asked the most

important reason I'm here yet."

"Because you're a king with no castle and needed a place to stay."

"Who says I don't have a kingdom?"

"You lived in a hole in the ground."

"For a short period in my life. I think when I get someone to write my memoirs, I am going to refer to those as my sabbatical years. A moment of peace before the real work started."

"And what's the real work? Are you serious about becoming king? Do you have any idea what kind of responsibility that might involve?"

"I don't fear work or even the fact the humans have started to move against us."

Following the direction of his mind proved fascinating, as he offered so many paths for her to explore. She stuck to one. "What do you mean the humans are moving on us?"

"That's not the most important issue facing me right now."

If the humans were preparing for war, then didn't they need to deal with it? "What could be more important?"

"Convincing you to accept me."

The statement stole whatever breath she might have had. It sounded so perfect, so true. And yet, she knew it was a lie.

She shoved away from him, and her hand cracked across his cheek.

He didn't flinch. He didn't even move. He sounded curious when he said, "What was that for?"

"For making me believe the bullshit line

about me being your treasure." For a moment in the pit, she'd believed it, and then, when he'd arrived, she'd almost forgotten the truth Anastasia had revealed.

"You are my treasure, angel. My one and only."

"Am I really? Because I hear you slept with other women." She planted a hand on her hip. "Did you think I wouldn't find out?"

"I didn't technically sleep with them." At her growl, he held up his hands in surrender. "Don't be angry at me. I shouldn't have to explain myself, but since you are obviously agitated, let me point out a few things, the first being those encounters happened during my forgetful time. I didn't know you existed."

"If I'm so damned important, you should have still subconsciously known."

"Just like you knew you weren't kissing the right man."

Shame flushed her cheeks. He had a point. They'd both done things with other people, never realizing something about it wasn't right. Not entirely true, she'd noticed the lack of buzz when they touched, just never understood what it meant.

Yet, now that they could be together, it still wasn't right. "I can't be your treasure. I can't be your anything. You saw how it was downstairs with those dragonesses. You're a big shot."

"They just want me for my body." He looked down. "More specifically, my seed." His gaze rose to meet hers. "You only ever wanted me for me."

True. But want wasn't enough. "Were you serious about making a run for king?"

"Maybe. If I don't, then that means Samael will be in charge, and given Anastasia's motives thus far have been less than pure, that probably isn't a good thing."

"Are you going to try and convince me that you now care about the world? What happened to screw everyone but myself?"

"Oh, it's still all about me. However, it does occur to me that I should take a more active role in what happens in the world. After all, our children will need a kingdom to inherit."

Her knees kind of buckled at that point.

Chapter Twenty-two

His sweet angel swooned, and Remiel graciously caught her. Then almost dropped her when she said, "I am not having your babies."

"Why not? They will be spectacular babies." The most stupendous children of all.

"For one thing, I'm young. Way too young to want to be a mother. I just got out of a prison, and I'm not about to shackle myself to a hearth again popping out kids. I want to see the world."

"So we'll have a nursemaid."

She glared at him.

"Two nursemaids?"

More glaring.

"Perhaps we could tour the world first and then begin the begetting of our line."

It didn't quite get rid of her expression. "You want babies so badly, then pick one of those single ladies downstairs. They looked more than eager for you."

"But I don't want them." Which sounded rather petulant, so he added, "I want you."

She sighed. "And I must be a moron because I want you, too."

"I knew you liked me."

Again, she sighed.

"You act as if that's a bad thing."

"Just thinking of all the complications."

"We'll hire people to solve them."

Her hands returned to her hips. "That's just it. You can't just hire people to handle everything. For a guy who was used to being alone, you seem rather ready to have others do your dirty work."

"A good king knows when to delegate."

"You're not a king."

"Yet."

"Declaring it doesn't make it so. There are rules to governing this country."

"Human rules." He waved a hand. "Those don't apply to me."

"I can't do this." She stalked out of the room, and before he could grasp her intent, she yelled, "He's in here."

In a flash, silver-haired women filled the space, their eyes flashing so many colors—violet and blue and brown in repose, green fire when their beast side rose to take a peek.

His angel—who was proving most stubborn—had thrown him to the eligible dragonesses. What cruelty. How could she do this to him? How could she leave him?

It only served to make him want her more. She was so unimpressed by his excellent Golden genes. Not swayed by his ardent words.

He ordered. She disobeyed. Wasn't there a rule somewhere about that not happening?

The very fact that he couldn't bend her to his will made him yearn even more.

But how to make her change her mind?

Court her, idiot. He would have to show his worthiness to her. Starting now, by proving no other woman held his interest.

As the chattering around him got to be too much, he pulled his reflection inward and slipped through the atoms and moments of time, past the grasping mamas and their daughters, who seemed to have multiplied since his arrival at the door.

He made his way down the stairs, planning to stalk Sue-Ellen, following her by the trace of her aura, only he was waylaid.

A prickling of awareness had him looking over his shoulder to see a man. A big man.

A *really* big man wearing a scowl who wasn't fooled by his cloak. "You dirty blond prick, you leave Sue-Ellen alone."

And then, Remiel met the man's fist up close and personal!

Chapter Twenty-three

I know that voice. Sue-Ellen popped her head out of the living room in time to see Remiel slump to the floor, courtesy of her brother's right hook.

"What did you hit him for?" she squeaked.

"I told you he wasn't getting you back." Brandon glared down at Remiel.

"That's not Samael; that's Remiel, his brother, you idiot." Moving quickly to Remiel's side, she dropped to the floor and placed his head on her thighs. She brushed his blond hair back and shot a look at her brother. "I can't believe you did this."

"Don't you give me that attitude. I'm your big brother. It's my job to protect you, and don't tell me you didn't need protecting. He obviously assaulted you. He's wearing your scent."

"Because we were kissing."

It wasn't just Brandon who gasped. Others were listening, as well.

Let them eavesdrop. Then they'll know he's mine.

"You kissed him?"

She angled her chin. "So what if I did? I'm a grown woman now."

Brandon shook his head. "Wrong. You're my little sister. As in no man will ever do dirty things with a boy's little sister. Thus it is my duty to kill him before he defiles you."

"Don't you dare."

"I have to. It's in the Big Brother Rule Book."

"There is no such thing, and besides, you seem to keep forgetting that this is Remiel, not Samael."

"Don't care. Neither of them is worthy of my baby sister."

Her lips quirked. She hadn't realized how much she missed her big brother until now. "You do realize by calling them unworthy you just insulted the entire Golden line."

He winked. "They're not the only Gold around."

"What's that supposed to mean?"

"It means," Brandon said, helping her to her feet as Remiel's body was carted off by too many willing hands, "that there is more than one Golden dragon who can make a claim to the throne."

"But the prophecy talks about the one foretold."

"They do, and until recently, everyone assumed it spoke of Samael. But does it? I mean, we're talking about some old words. Words spoken by someone probably enjoying an epic drug-induced hallucination. Think of it. How can having a certain color of Sept make a person a leader?"

"If color isn't most important, then what is? Brains? Wealth?"

"Actually, I was going to say balls, but yours are good answers, too. But probably most important of all is who has the bigger power base. Speaking of which, I think it's time you met my wife."

Brandon's wife? The Silvergrace daughter herself. Sue-Ellen felt a nervous urge to check her hair. What if her new sister-in-law hated her?

What if, after just being reunited with Brandon, his wife never let them see each other again?

What if…

"It's about time I got to meet my new sister." The arms attacked out of nowhere and hugged Sue-Ellen with bone-cracking firmness. They also lifted and shook her. "Look at you. You're tiny. Wait until Adi gets a hold of you."

"Who's Adi?"

"My sister."

Sue-Ellen's feet hit the floor, and she was finally treated to a peek at her brother's wife. She'd seen her once before from afar. A silver-haired beauty with the most amazing amethyst eyes, eyes that could freakishly glow with green fire.

If I'm really dragon, will mine glow like hers, too?

"You're Deka's cousin." She could see the resemblance.

"I am, but you're my new sister." Aimi clasped her hands. "How long until you make me an aunt?"

"A while. I'm not mated." And she never would be at this rate. Remiel wouldn't be happy with her brother.

"Really? I heard you claimed the newest Golden."

"No."

"In that case"—Aimi's lips curved—"you won't mind if I tell my unwed cousins."

"Remiel is free to be with whomever he chooses." If it was anyone other than Sue-Ellen, they'd die.

What?

Her inner self had only a cold chuckle as a reply.

"Speaking of Remiel, where have they taken him?" Sue-Ellen asked. She kept trying to act as if she didn't care, and yet, he consumed her thoughts constantly.

"They took him to Aunt Xylia's lab. While he's unconscious, she'll probably want to run tests on him."

"Tests as in taking blood and stuff?" Sue-Ellen's eyes widened. That wouldn't go over well. "I gotta go."

She'd better move quickly. She followed a trail that weaved through the mansion. It wasn't one of scent but more of instinct. She just knew where to go, as if a thread bound her to Remiel and she simply followed it back to the source.

She didn't move fast enough.

The floor underfoot trembled.

Uh-oh.

She ran faster.

Chapter Twenty-four

Remiel held the woman by the throat, his golden hands tipped in claws pressing against her skin.

How easy it would be to kill her. To slam her against the wall a few times. To toss her like a ball through that glass cabinet filled with jars. Or he could simply twist her head and pop it.

I hate doctors. Even pretty ones like the one he dangled in the air.

Imagine his surprise when he'd woken up in a clean bed. Imagine his greater surprise when he realized someone had clocked him hard enough to put him out.

Impressive and unacceptable. *I'll have to kill the person.*

First, though, he decided to murder the woman daring to stick him with a needle.

Which was why and how his angel found him a moment later when she ran into the room.

"Don't kill her. Put her down."

Instead, he stared at the woman, fury burning in his veins. "She wasss poking at me with a needle," he lisped.

"She wasn't doing it to harm you."

His angel placed her hands on his biceps,

and instantly her touch soothed. "I don't like needlesss." The s on the end rolled off his forked tongue.

"No one does, but that doesn't mean you get to be a big baby about it."

"Baby?" He turned to look at her over his shoulder. "Did you seriously call me an infant?" He set the woman down, releasing her before he fully turned.

"Well, you are whining an awful lot. Was it because she didn't offer you a lollipop?"

"Don't push me."

"I will push you if I damned well please. What are you going to do? Hit me?" She stood right in his face, and he could see she braced for it.

He wanted to kill something, but it most definitely wasn't her. "I would never harm you." Ever. *I'll kill anyone who does.*

"If I may speak, clan Silvergrace also didn't mean you any harm," added the older lady as she patted her hair. Her voice held a rasp.

"You don't mean me harm, and yet I was attacked in your home." Attacked and felled. Remiel would have to work harder so that it didn't happen again. He'd been lax in his studies and exercise.

The old lady's lips pursed. "That is our fault for not realizing Sue-Ellen's sibling would so quickly arrive."

Sibling? The big dude was related to his angel? Fuck. That probably meant no hitting back. "Why did you want samples if you don't mean me harm?"

"My sister, Waida, told us she'd met you, but

failed to get any genetic traces. We wanted to verify your claim."

"You want proof of who I am." Remiel smiled. He hoped it was his badass version. "Look into my eyes. See your proof." Whereas other dragons had a few shades of irises, all had green fire when the beast rose.

Except for Remiel. His eyes flashed gold.

"Remarkable," Xylia claimed. But instead of dropping to a knee to swear fealty, she whirled from him and tapped on a tablet on the table behind her, taking notes. "Is one of your special abilities speed healing your wounds?"

"More like years of practice being a punching bag." The doctors did so like to test his limits. He didn't mention it for sympathy, though, just simple truth. It backfired. He saw the pity on their faces and growled. "Don't feel sorry for me. It doesn't bother me." It hadn't in a while. Especially once he killed those who'd hurt him.

"Don't tell us how to feel. I will feel sorry for what they did because it's the right thing to do. No one should have hurt you that way." How fierce Sue-Ellen sounded. Always protecting him.

Just like I always protected her. But he couldn't protect her if he was a prisoner. The world might be coming after them. He needed an army. Now.

He veered his gaze to the silver-haired woman. He adopted his most serious mien. "I know you, Xylia Silvergrace. Sister to the matriarch, chief medical and science officer for the Silver Sept. You hold several degrees in biotechnology and chemistry, too. I see the reports of your underground lab weren't exaggerations."

"You're well informed."

"I didn't spend an idle childhood. Every waking hour was some kind of lesson." Back then, he and Samael had learned together. Their rivalry hadn't truly developed, and so they had supported each other. Quizzed each other that they might earn rewards. Until the day Samael betrayed him.

"I want to reiterate that, despite your past, now that we are aware of your existence, my liege is safe among the Silver Sept. As in the past, we are loyal to the Golden line and ready to give our pledge."

"Sounds good. So long as hooking up with the Silver families doesn't involve marriage. I'm already taken." When Sue-Ellen would have protested, he put a hand over her mouth. He smiled at Xylia. "She's shy about announcing it."

Xylia's gaze flicked to Sue-Ellen for a moment. "You might want to think about doing a mark that shows your commitment."

"Great idea and I'll take care of it as soon as you leave."

A chomp at his fingers had his hand pulling free, and Sue-Ellen exclaimed, "We aren't taking care of anything."

"Fine. I will do all the work, and you can enjoy it."

"You won't be—"

Since she wasn't being productive with her arguing, he covered her grumbles with a kiss. Since it didn't melt her tension, he kept kissing her. Then he kissed her just because he enjoyed it.

At one point during the kissing, Xylia left. *Finally alone.*

And did his woman appreciate it?

No!

She bit him and shoved away. "Don't think you can just kiss me and make this all go away."

"I was planning to do more than kiss."

"What if I don't want to be kissed?"

A slow smile pulled his lips. "You do." Said smugly since he could scent her arousal.

Her cheeks turned pink. "What my body wants and what I want are two very different things." She tossed her head. "There is too much baggage between us."

"I'll burn it."

"You can't be serious." She planted her hands on her hips, adorable in her anger. Annoying with her refusal to finally admit the truth.

"I am beyond serious. All my life, people have been playing games with me. Telling me what to do. Locking me up when I refuse. There is only one thing I've ever wanted in this world. Just one."

"To be free?"

"No. I only ever wanted you."

Her expression softened. "How can you say that after everything that has happened?"

"Because it's true. I see you and it's like the sun rises even if it's dark. I smell you and I feel a sense of rebirth, of hope. When I touch you..." He reached out and drew her near. "I feel alive."

"But—"

"There is no but," he said before silencing her with his lips. He pulled his angel close, deepening the embrace. To his groaning delight, she kissed him back, and her lips parted in acceptance. While his tongue went seeking, he molded her tightly against his body, leaving no space between them. Now if only they didn't wear clothes.

Then again, while Xylia had left, they could be interrupted at any moment.

Best to be quick. Lifting her in his arms, he brought her to the bed—which kind of looked like an old stone altar covered in white sheets.

His fingers threaded in her hair as he continued to kiss her while his other hand tugged at her pants, his hand sliding under the waistband and caressing her hip.

She moaned into his mouth, and her temperature rose.

He pulled his hand free and chose to join her on the bed. Her legs slid apart and seemed to welcome his weight nestling between them. Even through the layers of clothing, he could feel the heated core of her pressing against his erection. He rocked against her, applying even more pressure, and she gasped.

A hot pant of breath against his lips that kept stuttering with mewls of pleasure as he ground against her.

And this was just the beginning of the pleasure he'd give her.

He trailed his way across her jaw to the soft shell of her ear. He swirled his tongue and felt her digging her fingers into his sides, and her body trembled under him.

Slowly, he made his way down her neck to

the collar of her T-shirt. A T-shirt that stood in his way.

Rip.

Not anymore. He exposed his angel to his gaze. And under his fiery watch, her nipples hardened into nubs, nubs begging for his mouth.

Instead, he teased himself—and her—by rubbing his thumb over the tip of a nipple. Rub. Stroke. It tightened further, and her body quivered.

The peak called him. He bent and sucked it in, pulled as much of her breast as he could into his mouth. A guttural moan left her, a low, sexy sound of desire that only served to make his cock thicken even more.

He sucked her sweet berries, licking and nibbling her responsive flesh, loving how she bucked beneath him.

She made the most adorable mewling sounds. But only when she could breathe. More often, her breath caught as her head thrashed.

Her flushed skin oozed heat and sensuality, and he had to feel more of it.

Once more, his hand traveled downward, slipping past the waist of her pants. He dragged his fingers over the silk of her underpants. Then he slid a finger in. He ran it over her mound, feeling the short thatch arrowing to the apex of her thighs. He slipped his finger past it and sawed it over her damp lips.

Yes, damp. Wet for him.

He ran a few more fingers back and forth, feeling her shudder.

He could see and feel and even smell how

much she desired him, but he needed to hear it, too. To finally have her accept him aloud. "Do you want me to stop?"

She didn't reply but reached to him, grabbing him by the neck and drawing him down for a kiss. "Please, Remiel."

Please. He was the one who should be begging.

He definitely planned to worship. He shoved her pants down, giving him better access.

He let a finger slip between her intimate folds to dip into her honeypot. It dripped sweetness. It soaked his finger, and he used it to rub against her clitoris. Rubbed it only for a moment before she arched and cried out his name.

Her virgin body couldn't handle it. She came so quickly, but he wasn't done. He pinned her with his frame while keeping his hand between them, stroking.

She sobbed against his mouth as his hand continued to work its magic against her, dipping and rubbing, forcing her pleasure to build again. He kept touching her, feeling the heat and desire of her and yet having to be patient.

So patient. When she whimpered against his mouth, "Please, Remiel," he knew she was ready for him.

He quickly slid his pants past his hips, freeing him. He grabbed his erection one-handed while the other propped him over her.

The hardness of his shaft felt heavy in his grip, but he enjoyed the erotic feel as he rubbed the tip of his cock against her.

His angel gasped, and again she arched, sweet breasts poking into the air. He rubbed himself again, and again, making his cock slippery, driving her a little wild with lust.

When her eyes opened, the brown irises glowing with a strange yellow fire, he couldn't help but be captivated by them.

He kissed her with his eyes wide open. The head of him pushed at the entrance to her sex then stopped when he felt something in his way.

She spread wider for him, and her fingers dug into his waist. Her legs locked around him, and he felt himself pushing against her hymen but not quite tearing it.

Being a virgin meant pain for her this first time. He didn't want to do it. Couldn't hurt her. He paused, hovering above her, sweat gleaming on his skin as he hesitated.

"You can't stop now," she murmured against his lips.

"This will irrevocably join us." Much as he hated giving her the choice, he still did. Gave the choice even though all he wanted was to—

Apparently, Sue-Ellen didn't like his hesitation. Her legs locked tight, and her hands dragged him closer, pulling him into her body, her hips thrusting up, ramming him within her and sheathing him completely.

Holy fucking God.

It was a very religious moment. He was pretty sure angels sang. He definitely felt lightning hit, a flash that left him more hyper-aware of Sue-Ellen than ever.

He didn't need to ask if she felt it, too. He already knew she did, sensing it through this new bond, which was how he knew she was okay—and ready for more.

His lips clinging to hers, he began to move, hips thrusting and grinding as he pushed into her and pulled back. Sliding and stretching her, feeling her tight all around him and tightening further as she got closer to the peak. He was skirting to the edge himself, and each thrust brought him closer. Closer.

When she nipped his lip, sharp enough to break skin, his cock swelled and burst, forcing him deep one last time and triggering a scream from his angel, followed by dick-crushing waves of pleasure as her channel reacted. It pulsed around him, wringing every last ounce of pleasure from him that it could.

Wrung out and sated, he almost collapsed on top of his angel. He managed to brace his arms enough that he didn't crush her with his full weight. Her eyes were shut, and her lips parted as she recovered. He rubbed his mouth over hers, and she sighed, a happy sound.

"That was epic."

"You're epic," he said with a soft snort. "And mine."

"As if I wasn't before."

"But now it's official." His throbbing lower lip proclaimed it. Just like his tearing of her maidenhead had claimed her. Blood for blood to join them for a lifetime.

"Officially complicated," she grumbled, but

spoken with the sweetest of smiles. Her hand reached out to stroke his cheek. Through the bond they shared, he felt her absolute contentment. Happiness.

Love.

She loved him just as he loved her. As if he could ever doubt. Awesomeness like him hadn't been seen in centuries.

Still sheathed inside her tight, wet body, his shaft hardened again. He'd waited so long to be with her that just once wouldn't be enough. A lifetime might never be enough.

But for now, at least, round two would have to wait. For one thing, she had been a virgin. Her female parts were probably sore, and here he was still buried inside her. He withdrew and rolled to his side.

She growled. Quite loudly. "Where do you think you're going?"

"To kill whoever is about to interrupt us."

Too late.

The door crashed open, and a silver-haired girl popped her head in.

"Yo, Suzie. We've got company." The girl retreated, only to poke her head back in to wink at him and exclaim, "Nice ass."

"She's going to die." He would note it wasn't him that threatened that but Sue-Ellen.

"Who is it?" he asked, rolling off the bed completely and pulling up his breeches.

"That's Deka Silvergrace."

"Her new BFF," exclaimed Deka, once again popping in. "You need to move it, love dragons.

The Crimson matriarch slash priestess of the Gold is here demanding audience, and Aunt Yolanda is being super nice, which is really scary."

"Hold on. Did you say Crimson matriarch? Since when?" Remiel asked.

"Since the previous Crimson leader croaked along with all but one of the daughters. The one that's left is underage, so the priestess stepped in as guardian and is now controlling the Crimson Sept. And now she thinks she's hot shit since she showed up without an appointment, making demands."

"What kind of demands?" he asked as he finger combed his hair.

"She says you're betrothed and is insisting you fulfill the terms of that bargain."

"She wants you to get married?" Sue-Ellen screeched, and he laughed at the rage he felt through their bond.

Jealousy suited her.

Chapter Twenty-five

Good thing Remiel caught her around the waist because, for a moment, Sue-Ellen kind of lost her shit.

Betrothed? Who was the hussy who thought to sink her claws into Sue-Ellen's man?

"You can calm yourself, angel. I am not betrothed. If they're claiming anything, then it was done under duress without my consent."

Deka leaned against the doorjamb and jerked a thumb at the hall. "Well, you might want to explain that to them because she's here, and she didn't come alone."

"My brother is with her?" His expression brightened.

"Yes, he is. Think you can put in a good word for me?" Deka replied.

"I'll go, but you stay here and guard Sue-Ellen. I don't want Anastasia anywhere near her."

With that imperious demand, he strolled out the door. Thinking he could make decisions for her.

Ha. Not likely.

Sue-Ellen scowled as she wiggled her pants back up over her hips. "Why, that arrogant idiot. Acting like he's the boss of me. Going off by himself, with no plan of action. He's going to get himself killed."

"Killed? Not likely. Right now, he's a hot commodity. Accidentally married on the other hand? High possibility."

"Like hell is he getting married." Remiel was already claimed, and now that it had happened, she could totally defend it.

Despite his order, there was no question of Sue-Ellen staying behind. Not with Remiel possibly in danger.

Deka made no move to stop Sue-Ellen from leaving Xylia's lab, but the Silvergrace girl did feel a need to run a commentary as they followed Remiel to the main floor. "Looks like someone got deflowered, and by a king no less. Should we hang the royal sheets from the walls that all the Septs might know of your union?"

Cheeks hot, she grumbled, "I'm going to hang you if you say a word to anyone."

"A word about what?" Brandon asked, having heard them as he came down the stairs.

"Nothing." Said a little too fast by Sue-Ellen, but that wasn't what gave her away. Her brother sniffed the air. His brow wrinkled. His lips pursed, and small hands gripped him around the biceps. He didn't seem to notice as he raised his arm, lifting his wife.

"He's dead," he growled.

"Don't you dare touch him!" Sue-Ellen yelled. "I mean it. He didn't do anything to me that I didn't want."

"I heard the moaning. She's not kidding," Deka added to help the situation.

"I don't want to hear this!" Brandon stuck fingers in his ears and sang, "La. La. La."

Aimi had given up holding his arm and, instead, leaned against the wall, laughing. "And I thought my family was entertaining."

Sue-Ellen had more important things to worry about than her brother's misplaced sense of chivalry. Sue-Ellen was a grown woman, and as such, she had no problem stalking past her brother—and throwing a cheap shot to his groin that had him gasping for air.

She bolted past him and up the remaining steps, following that now much thicker thread between her and Remiel.

She tracked it to a hall showcasing gray slate floors and white plaster walls. The silver sconces held no light, as daylight streamed through the windows. It helped illuminate the crowd gathered outside the huge double doors, ears pressed, listening.

Listening to what?

Deka elbowed her way to the front and dragged Sue-Ellen with her. In no time, Sue-Ellen's ear was pressed against the smooth and cool surface, straining to pick up sound.

She first heard a female murmur. Then a barked, "Not likely." Remiel didn't sound pleased. But Sue-Ellen was because she distinctly heard him declare, "I'm already claimed, so you can forget your matchmaking plans."

The heat of his words bathed her with pleasure, and she couldn't help a stupidly large smile—*he chose me.*

Of course, that meant that something just had to go wrong. The house suddenly went silent as the power went out, and for a moment, not a sound could be heard, not even a single person taking a breath.

Anticipation had no noise.

In the stillness, nobody could miss the *whup-whup-whup* of a helicopter approaching. But of more immediate concern was the glass that started shattering because bullets were being fired!

Chapter Twenty-six

The tinkling glass sent Remiel to the floor.

Zahra barked, "Who is attacking? How come we didn't get any warning?"

His fault. He might have knocked out some of the defense systems on his way into the manor. They were in his way.

Besides, one did not deny a king entrance, especially not when he came seeking the sum of his existence.

"Does it matter how they got onto the property?" grumbled Yolanda.

The Silver matriarch crouched behind her desk, and her eyes glowed green. "How dare they invade my territory." With that ominous growl, Zahra ran for the shattered patio doors and dove through, a blur of woman, shredding fabric, and glinting silver.

Looked like fun. Remiel wasn't averse to joining her, especially since he wanted answers, but he didn't need to go outside to get those.

He reached out and grabbed Samael by the collar and dragged him close before demanding, "Why are your men attacking?"

"Are you fucking deluded? This isn't my doing. I'm being shot at, too."

Good point. A glance at the scowling Anastasia huddling behind a table she'd overturned made it pretty clear she hadn't orchestrated this either.

Who did that leave?

Do the humans dare attack us on the Silvers' grounds?

The distinct percussion of a helicopter rotor got louder, and as black-combat-clad figures dashed toward the house, spilling from invisible blinds— the magical kind he'd not known existed until this moment—bodies also rappelled from the sky.

The house was under a full-scale attack. How epic.

What fun.

As king, it fell on him to help defend the manor.

And yet…as Remiel dove out the window and went after the first idiot to point a gun, he noted, for all the flashiness of the attack, it was also a rather futile one.

He grabbed the rifle from the fellow in black combat gear and tore it from his human grip. Before he could demand answers, the body convulsed and collapsed, leaving Remiel to stand over the body. He wasn't the only one sorely disappointed.

A sea of silver poured out of the house and burst into their primal shapes. Sinuous bodies, glittering scales, sharp talons, and wings filled the sky. They trilled as they hunted, proved beautifully deadly as they struck, shredding the attacking enemy until only one remained. One sniveling human held in the grip of Remiel's brother.

"Who sent you?" Samael shook the human, and this time, Remiel caught the glint of something in its mouth. His brother must have seen it, too, because he tilted the human and pounded him on the back until something shot free. A capsule.

Want to bet it's full of poison?

Someone didn't want them to get any answers.

Too bad.

Unsatisfied by the fight, Remiel had little patience for the weasel who still refused to answer Samael.

Remiel tore the attacker from his brother's grip, tossed him in the air, and watched him land before asking, "Who sent you to kill me?"

"What he meant to say," Samael interjected, "was who sent you to kill me? The rightful king."

Lying on his back, the human, stinking of his own mortality, grinned through bloody teeth. "The true leader is coming. Pretenders must die." Ridiculous claim made, the human shoved his hand against his mouth. In but a second, he began to bubble, literally. Froth poured from his mouth and dribbled down his chin, and his eyes bulged, the veins in them popping a moment before the eyeballs themselves exploded.

Remiel kept his lips clamped and wiped an arm across his face before saying, "I need a drink."

Actually, he'd needed a drink from the first moment he stepped into Zahra's office and saw Anastasia standing by Samael's side. Their presence here could only be a trap.

The good news? Neither looked pleased.

The bad news? The Silver matriarch probably wouldn't appreciate the blood on her white marble. The stains proved almost impossible to remove.

Remiel rubbed his hands together. "To what do I owe the displeasure of this visit? Don't tell me. Samael is here to kneel to the rightful king and beg my brotherly forgiveness, and you've decided to set yourself on fire in atonement for your existence."

"I came here looking for Sue-Ellen. I didn't know *she* would be coming." Samael glared at Anastasia.

"That juvenile attitude is why you can't be king," sniffed the priestess. "Speaking of whom, you"—she jabbed a red-manicured finger at Remiel—"have a promise to keep."

Zahra, also present and keeping a watchful eye and ear, asked, "What promise?"

Yolanda, wearing glasses perched on the tip of her nose, raised her head from a laptop to add, "Keep in mind, any promise verbally made under a certain age is not legally binding."

Anastasia looked much too pleased. "The king is betrothed. As his guardian, I arranged it. Nothing illegal about it."

"I didn't agree, and it's just not happening." Remiel shrugged. "Sorry you came all this way. Do let the door hit you on the way out."

"No matter your opinion of me, you cannot shirk your duty."

"I'm not shirking my duty. As a matter of fact, I took care of the begetting of the heir part only moments ago." He made sure to grin at his brother.

Samael's peeved expression said he caught the implication.

So did Anastasia. "A pity you wasted your seed, but now that you've gotten the girl out of your system, you can do what's right for the Sept."

"You mean what's right for *your* Sept," Zahra objected.

The Crimsons' idea of right for the Sept and the Silvers' one, while similar—marry within the family—had one major flaw.

Remiel was already claimed.

He came back to the moment and the futile carnage. Why attack? Surely they'd known they couldn't win.

Wiping his hands, Samael, who, like his brother, had never bothered to change shape, moved closer. "Is it me, or do these attacking humans seem to have an element of crazy to them?"

"You mean more than usual?"

"Humans don't usually commit suicide like that. Not without a cause."

"No, they don't." The question of why they attacked remained unclear.

"Do the humans wish to start a war with us?" Samael spoke mostly to Remiel. Any feud between them seemed suddenly paused or forgotten as a graver danger faced them.

If his brother thought he could be a big man, then Remiel would show him he could be bigger. "A handful of misguided humans do not make for a conspiracy on a global level."

"It also doesn't mean the humans are entirely behind it. The dragons have many enemies," Yolanda noted, having approached their little group, along with the Silver matriarch, who'd managed to procure a robe to cover herself.

"Who could it be?" Zahra asked. "We've no quarrels with any other groups."

"Does it matter?" Anastasia seethed as she stalked toward them, the gore coating her making parts of her red ensemble darker in spots. "These human infidels attacked us."

"And we took care of it." Samael gestured. The cleanup had already begun.

"We need to do more than that. They will try again."

"What do you suggest we do?" Zahra asked. Despite her lack of a silver suit, the robe did not deter from her sneer at all. "We can't exactly go to war with the humans. There are billions to our thousands."

"Only a fraction would actually fight," Remiel observed, bending down to look at the body. He lifted a hand. "Anyone recognize this symbol he's wearing?" He lifted the medallion that had fallen from the neck of his shirt. The symbol on it nagged with familiarity.

"Whatever club they belong to won't exist for long. Its days are numbered. We can't have outsiders attacking the potential king," Zahra declared.

"Kings," Samael amended. "There are two of us."

"Three if you count the freak Parker made." Anastasia just couldn't help herself.

"Don't you mean four?" Deka, who kept popping up, added to the conversation.

"Who's the fourth?" Anastasia asked.

But Remiel suddenly could guess. Because if one Mercer had managed to make the flip to partial Gold, then…

He frowned at Deka. "Weren't you supposed to be guarding Sue-Ellen?"

"I was, but then she insisted we check things out, and well, she does technically outrank me."

"Where is she? She wasn't harmed in the attack?"

"Harmed?" Deka snorted. "Not even close. Brand and Aimi whisked her off while you guys were playing."

"Where has he taken her?" Samael asked, and Remiel whirled on him.

"Why do you want to know? I already told you she's mine."

"For the moment. How long do you think a widow needs to grieve?"

"Are you threatening me?" Remiel stood tall next to Samael. But they were both the same height. Almost the same weight. It would be an epic battle.

Remiel cracked his knuckles. He'd waited a long time for this moment. "What do you say, brother? Shall we finish this once and for all?"

"Boys! Enough." The rebuke rang with command, and the boys turned to look at Zahra. Their matching expressions conveyed a clear "Excuse me?"

"While your posturing is most entertaining, you are wasting your time and energy fighting each other when we have much graver problems to handle."

"I don't know about you, but since Sue-Ellen's safe with her big bro for the moment, then I've got time to teach my little brother here a lesson."

Fingers lifted and beckoned. "My calendar is also pretty clear," Samael said.

The fists lifted again, and matching grins, fierce ones, split their lips as they dropped into a stance.

"Idiots. You're idiots. Don't you see? Someone came after you both and didn't care how public they were about it. This is more important than any feud."

Anastasia grimaced. "I have to agree with the old hag. But not for the same reason. These humans are obviously part of a cult that doesn't mind killing its members. They are but minor irritants, easily subdued. What you should worry about is the fact that Brandon took the girl. Don't you see what this means?"

"He loves his sister?"

"He wants to keep her safe?"

"No!" Anastasia practically screeched. "Think, you idiots. Why would Brandon take the mate of a Golden king?"

"Possible king," Samael interjected.

Remiel got the answer first, although the mental leap took a bit because of the temerity of the thought. "You think Brandon's going to attempt to take my throne and use Sue-Ellen as a bargaining chip with the Septs."

Oh, hell no. The throne and angel were his, and his alone.

Time to get her back.

He wasn't the only one who got that idea. One moment, Samael stood with them; the next, he'd vanished.

"That bastard." Remiel cast out his senses and caught a hint of his brother's aura as he fled under a guise of invisibility.

Remiel's plan to tackle Samael was stopped by a hand on his arm.

Remiel stared at the fine-skinned fingers that dared halt him.

Zahra didn't remove them, nor did she apologize for her temerity. "Let the boy go. We know where he flees, and Brandon won't let him near the girl."

"Samael won't be a problem once I get my claws around his neck."

"You can't kill him." It wasn't Anastasia but Zahra that spoke. "The Golds are too few and precious to waste over petty squabbles."

"Petty? He kept me in a pit."

"And?" Zahra eyed him. "You don't seem as if you've suffered."

"Pretty princess," Deka coughed into a fist.

"He is challenging my right to rule."

"Are you not strong enough to withstand it?"

"I am." His chest puffed out. "But I shouldn't have to constantly defend. Not when there's an easier solution."

"What if I had something better than death?"

As Remiel listened to the Silver matriarch's plan, he grinned. Then laughed.

Once he agreed to it, he left to find his angel.

My queen.

Chapter Twenty-seven

"You're going to *what?*" Sue-Ellen screeched, not for the first time. She'd done lots of screeching since her brother had plucked her from the chaos of breaking glass and shooting bullets. He'd tucked her under an arm, along with his wife, who insisted, "We should stay for the fight."

"That's not a fight," Brandon replied. "It's a diversion. And we're going to take advantage of it." Her brother then proceeded to take Sue-Ellen to an armored Hummer parked in the garage and sped out of there with squealing tires, with Aimi behind the wheel. Bats in Hell had nothing on her new sister-in-law. Apparently, speed limits were for peasants.

"I said I am going to declare myself king." Brandon paced the living room of the condo he and Aimi had borrowed. Aunt Waida was apparently still out of town. "Don't you see? It makes the most sense."

"No, I don't see. You aren't a king. You're not even royalty. You used to run around the bayou diaperless when you were young because Ma couldn't afford to buy any butt covers."

"And you used to eat caterpillars. That didn't stop Remiel from making you part of his hoard."

"How did you hear about that?"

Brandon rolled his eyes. "Did you really think I wouldn't find out?"

"Your information is a little off. I am not simply part of his treasure; I am his one and only treasure." Because he loved her. Through the bond tying them together, she could feel his worry—and annoyance.

It won't be long now before he comes to find me.

The thought filled her with warmth, but her brother tried to douse it.

"You're his one and only treasure?" He sounded aghast. "Does he know you're the girl who won the burping alphabet contest three years in a row?"

Those were the types of things a girl didn't put on a resume—and she'd kill Brandon if he ever told Remiel about it.

Speaking of whom… "Are you sure Remiel is safe?" Because in the commotion, she couldn't be sure. Being tossed upside down over an overprotective brother's shoulder tended to do that. The tie linking them didn't radiate any pain, but Remiel, being a man, wouldn't necessarily make it obvious.

"I don't think your beau needs any help," Brandon grumbled.

"How do you know that?"

"Because I'm pretty sure he just landed on the rooftop across from us."

She ran to the window for a peek.

A Golden dragon was definitely perched across the way. But it wasn't pure gold, and nothing tugged at her. Not in that direction. "That's not Remiel."

"Is it the other pretender? I've been wanting to talk to him, too. Nice of him to put himself within reach." Brandon cracked his knuckles.

"You will not kill him."

"I heard what he did. The guy is a psycho."

"He is, but…" She bit her lip. Samael also remained Remiel's brother. A man who'd spent his life manipulated. Could anyone really blame him for what had happened?

She hesitated too long.

Sliding the patio door open, Brandon launched himself out of the opening, changing midleap.

Sue-Ellen turned an astonished face on Aimi. "Aren't you going to stop him?"

"Why would I do that? He wants to be all big and macho, then let him. He is part Gold. Asserting dominance is in their blood. You have to admit Brand would make a good choice for king."

The throne is rightfully Remiel's. The words almost passed her lips, but she stopped them.

What was happening? How had the dragons gone from no kings to too many? And why were they fighting for the throne?

Because he who rules the Septs is all-powerful.

If only she had that power. Having it meant no one telling her what to do anymore. No one trying to hurt Remiel. No one ever doing anything to their children—because, yes, they would eventually have children, and those children would have to be protected.

They will be my treasure. For a moment, she saw the world in shades of green and gold. Then she blinked and the sensation was gone.

A knock at the door saw her whirling, especially since it was a precursor to the door being blown off its hinges by a powerful strike.

Over the debris he'd created stepped Remiel. He brushed at the dust trying to cling and strode directly toward her, his laser stare intent. He looked dangerous and strong.

Mine.

"Angel."

She smiled. "Took you long enough." She'd felt his approach but didn't dare let Brandon know.

"I was making some deals with the Silver matriarch." He stopped a few paces from her.

"What kind of deals?" Because her understanding was the Silver Sept was looking for male dragons of breeding age. Males like Remiel.

"Let's just say that Samael is going to be a little too busy to bother you for the next while, given I've decided to let him live."

Her brows rose. "Does this mean you reconciled?"

"Never." His eyes flared gold. "But if he's fighting off dragonesses who want to be princesses, then he'll be too busy to harass you."

"Until someone nails him down." Deka came to mind. "And then he might come after your throne again."

"Then I'll deal with him."

"Deal how?"

"We'll discuss it later. Let's leave before your

brother comes back."

"My brother is kind of busy wrestling yours." She pointed to the window just as a pair of dragons swooped past.

"And winning," Aimi added from her spot peeking out.

"Time for us to leave." He held out his hand. A hand that, if taken, would mean giving up her newfound freedom and becoming a part of the chaos life with Remiel would entail.

It didn't require any real thought. Sue-Ellen had made her choice years ago.

Her fingers curled around his. "Where are we going?"

"To rule the world."

With that declaration, they both vanished from sight, leaving behind an exclaiming Aimi as they ran from the condo.

"Since when can you become invisible?" she asked, thinking the words and pushing them at the thread that bound them.

"Since I watched how my brother did it. It is but one of the feats a Gold can do."

It proved helpful in getting them to the stairwell unnoticed and past the gawkers peeking from the other condos on that level. They went up instead of down, Remiel choosing the rooftop to make their escape.

Only the rooftop wasn't empty. Not by a long shot.

"Stay hidden."

Remiel shimmered into view, and yet, somehow, Sue-Ellen remained invisible. He released her hand and took a step forward, partially covering her invisible body.

The rigid lines of his frame went with the firm emotion emanating from him. Caution.

Anastasia stood at the head of a group of wyverns. Regal and arrogant, just like her words. "Remiel D'Ore, will you come to your senses? Will you honor the pledge made in your name to bind yourself to the Crimson Sept and make a princess into a queen?"

Remiel sneered. "Don't you mean false princess? We all know that, while the Crimson matriarch might have stylized herself as queen, her blood has no claim to royalty."

"Her ranking matters not. The blood of the Crimson Sept heir is pure. Any children born of that union would be—"

"Half-breeds." Remiel cocked his head. "Because she is just a Red."

"Just?" Anastasia's lips tightened. "The Crimson is the most powerful of the Septs."

"Yeah, I'd kind of have to disagree with that." Aimi sauntered into view, her silver hair streaming past her shoulders, her eyes flashing with green fire. "The Silvers have always been second in line to the throne."

"Your Sept has grown weak," Anastasia snapped.

"And you're deluded," Remiel interjected. "I am already mated, and to one greater than any of the Septs can offer."

"The girl is an abomination." The words spat from Anastasia, and Sue-Ellen—still hidden—

had to hold in a gasp as the priestess's eyes flashed. Not green. Nor even the gold she'd seen Remiel sport.

But red. A malevolent ring of fire.

"What have you done?" Remiel spoke the words softly.

"Done?" Anastasia laughed and took a step forward, her crimson gown undulating. Unnaturally.

Where did that extra ripple come from?

"Your scent is wrong."

"Ah, yes. The animals and their sense of smell." A slender hand waved, and the sleeve fell, revealing the thin wrist and the swirling tattoos crawling up the forearm. Tattoos Sue-Ellen didn't recognize. Had Anastasia been covering them all this time?

"You are not the priestess," Remiel stated. "Who are you? Show your true self."

"Clever little Golden dragon. You have found me out." She clasped a hand to her breast, a breast that shimmered and went from a voluptuous woman in red silk to something tall, shrouded in a cloak.

A shadow overhead made a thump as it landed. Another soon followed. Samael and Brandon had taken note of the confrontation and now stood at their back. Sue-Ellen should have taken comfort in them, especially given how fierce they were wearing a dragon suited for fighting.

But...the confidence of the cloaked one proved unnerving.

And the red eyes... What did they mean? Who was it?

Samael raised a claw and pointed before uttering a high trill. The wyverns clustered around the figure stiffened. They hesitated, but only for a moment. In the absence of their mistress, they could not deny the command of a Gold.

They might as well have thrown meat at a moving scythe. The fluid grace and blurring quickness of the cloaked figure meant the wyverns never stood a chance. A pair of long blades emerged from voluminous sleeves.

The dull surfaces didn't reflect as they sliced and diced, leaving the poorly equipped squadron of beasts in pieces on the tarred and pebbled surface.

As soon as it began, it ended. The blades suddenly retreated into the billowing material, and the cloaked one folded arms in front. "I do hope that wasn't your best shot."

Bodies suddenly flowed forward, several of them. Remiel, who pulled at his dragon, the golden scales rippling past his fleshy skin. Brandon dashed, wings tucked tight to his back. Even Aimi soared past, silver gleaming scales catching the light.

All of them, even Samael, caught midflight, froze with a wave of a hand. All them formed a silent mannequin challenge, frozen in place. No one breathing, blinking, or flexing a muscle.

"Before you attack, perhaps I should show you something. I have a gift for the new king and his future queen."

"What gift?" Remiel spoke through stiff lips, even if he couldn't move.

"The gift of a smooth transition. Behold, your greatest enemy." Dangling from a fist, the hand gripping red locks, her expression frozen in surprise, was Anastasia. Or at least part of her.

"You killed the priestess of the Gold and the acting head of the Crimson Sept," Remiel stated.

"You're welcome."

"I didn't ask for it."

"And yet it is my gift to you."

"What do you want?"

"Want?" The words emerged on a streaming flute of notes, the pitch lilting up and down, feminine yet gruff. "I want nothing more than to congratulate the couple on their nuptials. But you seem rudely determined to refuse my gift." The gloved fingers holding the red hair of the priestess released the head, and it fell with a meaty *thunk*. Still, no one moved. Not a single muscle. Even Sue-Ellen, in her invisible blind, didn't dare twitch. She remained hidden and held her breath because she felt the coldness radiating from the figure. The evil.

"Mark this day." The words emerged from the dark shroud, soft and yet so powerful, neither truly male nor female. "On this day, the end of everything begins. The prophecy of the Gold enters its second phase. Humanity's time, dragons' mortality…all is now measured only by grains of sand sifting through the hourglass of time."

There was probably some real deep message in there, some kind of reasoning to the craziness that popped out of nowhere.

Sue-Ellen didn't care. In that robed figure, she saw danger, not just to herself but to everyone she loved.

Running on stealthy feet, she made not a

sound, and yet the person in the cloak still heard her and stared right at Sue-Ellen. Eyes ringed in red fire peered from the depths of the cowl. One single upraised hand was all it took.

Whump. The blast to Sue-Ellen's chest swept her off her feet. Right over the edge of the building.

Did she mention there was no net?

No Remiel or Deka to swoop in and save her.

Still no freaking parachute.

I don't need no stinking parachute. I have wings. The coldness in her begged, "*Let me out.*"

The wildness in her pulsed. It promised power. Would grant her strength. Would keep her from splattering her guts onto the pavement.

She took it.

Her skin rippled. Stretched. Ohmygod, did it stretch. Her body became lighter, bigger, and lighter still. Everything in her crackled, but the pain proved fleeting and euphoric.

When it was done…she was a bloody dragon and, despite her wings, still falling!

Chapter Twenty-eight

Remiel pretended to freeze like the others, mostly so he could observe the stranger. Perhaps get a hint as to their identity.

But the smell was like nothing he'd ever encountered. The aura like nothing he'd ever seen—swirling smoke.

The power was vast, and a lesser being would be affected. Not a Gold. Which was why Sue-Ellen could probably move and thought to take matters into her own hands.

She'd failed. Whoever they faced had magic, a magic that wasn't dragon or anything he'd seen, heard of, or been taught.

As Sue-Ellen found herself magically shoved off the building, he was faced with a choice. Save Sue-Ellen or the world?

The person in the cloak presented a clear and present danger to him and his kind.

Sue-Ellen was just one person.

As with all decisions in his life, there was only one answer.

He dove off the parapet after his angel and thus saw the moment that she finally made that connection with the dragon that had somehow found its way inside of her. He saw her explode into a fabulous golden beast of epic size and beauty, her scales lined in edges of green, a hint of her bayou heritage. Her wings unfurled from her back, mighty sails of thin gossamer. He saw the panic in her eyes as she fluttered them but still fell.

"They don't work!"

He heard her mental screech of annoyance and almost smiled. *"Don't worry, angel. I won't let you fall."* He'd never let her fall.

He dove, wings tight to his back, arrowing toward her and reaching out.

"Grab my hands."

"Paws?"

"Whatever." He caught her and flipped them midair so she was on top. Then he instructed her.

"Extend your wings all the way."

One opened right up; the other wobbled.

"Both of them."

"I'm trying."

"Try harder."

"Bully." A complaint, and yet she did as told. Snap. The second wing fully extended, and she caught some air. He kept her atop him, though, his own wings bearing the brunt of the work, but not for much longer.

"Get ready to flap, but stay in this wind stream." He let go of her and flipped over that he might show her by example.

Elation pulsed through his link with her.

"It's working."

"As if there was any doubt. Dragons are meant to fly."

"I'm flying." A sense of wonder filled the link

between them.

Indeed, she finally flew, but the lesson took a few too many moments, and by the time they returned to the rooftop, the cloaked figure was gone. The priestess was still headless, and Aimi was on the phone, probably calling a cleanup crew to start on the mess. Meanwhile, Brandon held Samael in a headlock.

Landing, Remiel managed to brace enough to keep Sue-Ellen from rolling.

"I can't believe I'm a clumsy dragon," she grumbled as he caught her.

"You just need practice."

"Practice being a fucking dragon." Her majestic head shook, the silken spines on her mane shimmering. *"I'm a dragon."*

"I know, angel." A beautiful one, too.

"Does the gold thing mean we're related?"

A good question. There weren't many Gold choices around, and later that day, Xylia actually answered it as they held a sudden war room meeting to discuss what had happened.

All four Goldens had been invited, although Samael was under guard so he wouldn't try any tricks. Remiel almost felt sorry for him, especially when Deka muttered, "Don't worry, Remi"—her nickname for him—"I'll keep an eye on the evil overlord. He won't escape me."

He almost laughed at the look of fear in Samael's eyes.

No one objected when Waida arrived to lead the meeting, but she didn't add much to the conversation other than to say, yes, there was a building movement amongst the humans against dragons and other cryptos. Yes, there was a lot of interest in kidnapping or controlling the newly emerged Golds, but not for power. The humans wanted their genes.

Xylia explained. "Somehow, the human scientists have discovered that the essence from a Gold can help ease mutations in humans without the insanity. But the more interesting thing is the results of the blood work. While Remiel and Samael are definitely related, their Golden gene is not the same as that carried by the Mercer branch."

"So we're not brother and sister?" Sue-Ellen asked. "Thank God."

"Whose Golden essence do they carry, then?"

No one had the answer to that question.

Just like no one knew who the hell had been in that cloak.

"Surely the histories mention a race with red eyes?" Remiel snapped back at the mansion.

Aunt Xylia shook her head. "None. The dragons are green."

"And gold," Remiel amended.

"The shifters shine yellow. The faeries are amethyst."

"What of the merpeople?" he asked.

"The dull darkness of kelp from the deepest reaches." Xylia spread her hands. "I know not of any race with fiery eyes."

"The humans do." All eyes turned to Yolanda.

"Explain," commanded Zahra.

"You just need to read one of their bibles to find it. Demons."

"Don't exist," exclaimed Xylia.

"Neither did we, supposedly."

The taunting rejoinder began a tedious back and forth that led nowhere.

The meeting lasted several hours, and all that was accomplished was Brandon agreeing to back down on his claim as king—too much work, he claimed—if Remiel was truly serious about making Sue-Ellen his wife.

Samael objected to Remiel keeping Sue-Ellen, to which Deka took offense. No one was surprised when he managed to escape during a break. Nor was anyone surprised when Deka didn't return after. What did cause shock was her returning empty-handed—and not happy about it.

With his emotions conflicted about his brother, Remiel let Samael flee for now. Remiel had more important things to attend to, such as securing the position of his future queen.

This time, he chose a bed for his actions.

When everyone called it a night, Remiel took that opportunity to spirit Sue-Ellen to her bedroom. It wasn't the grand suite deserving of a queen, but it would do for now.

Shutting the door behind him, he opened his mouth and found it attacked by Sue-Ellen. Ferociously attacked.

"Finally succumbing to my greatness," he remarked."

"Just glad you're alive." Said with a lick of his lower lip.

"As if there were any question."

"Somehow, I'm alive, despite getting tossed from a roof."

"I'd never let anything happen to you." Ever.

"Looks like we're still in danger."

"That goes without saying."

She placed her palms on his chest. "I love you."

Of course she did. "I've always loved you." He would only ever love her. For this woman, his angel, this king would kneel. He dropped to a knee, but he forwent a flowery speech.

"Would you do me the honor of being my mate?"

"Shouldn't you have asked that before you seduced me?" she asked. "And before you told the dragons I was yours? And before you bargained with my brother?"

"Would the answer have changed?"

"No." She knelt in front of him and cupped his cheeks. "From the first time I saw you, I knew you were the one. And now that we're finally together…"

"…nothing can keep us apart."

The promise rang between them, and it might have carried its own form of magic——a lusty kind—because they tore at each other right after, their teeth clacking as their lips mashed together.

Theirs was a passion that would never subside.

Like a fire, it would only grow stronger. And lucky him, Sue-Ellen seemed determined to fuel that lust.

"Lie down for me. Hands behind your head."

Chapter Twenty-nine

Sue-Ellen couldn't have said where she got the nerve to order him around. But she did. She pushed him flat on his back and straddled him. She leaned over far enough that her breasts could brush his chest, and her lips teased his.

"I think we're wearing too much clothing," she said in a purr.

"I agree." He proceeded to rend her clothes from her body and his, the ripping of cloth exciting and a reminder that their palace would need a large and well-stocked closet if this was going to become a habit.

"The biggest you want," he agreed, the fact that he could read her so easily no longer a frightening prospect. It was only right that her mate understand her so well.

The hot hardness of his shaft poked at her backside, and she took a moment to almost purr as she rubbed against him, the skin-to-skin contact making her gasp in delight.

So much for her to discover, starting with a very insistent stick. Sliding down to straddle his thighs, she took him in a tight grip.

He gasped. She liked the sound so much she tightened her hand around him and experimented by stroking him up and down.

His hips quivered. All of him shuddered, actually. What fun. But what if she tasted him?

She dipped her head, and he bellowed her name at the first flick of her tongue. It only emboldened her to suck him further, pulling his mushroomed head into her mouth and sucking. Being a virgin until recently didn't mean she had no idea what sex involved.

It was nice finally being able to try it.

But Remiel wasn't content to just let her play. Her wrestled her around until they were on the bed and he had her straddling him, facing his feet. Since she still got to lick and play, she didn't mind, although when his lips touched her for the first time, she almost bit him.

It was close. She probably left teeth marks on his shaft. Then again, it was his fault. The wet swipe of his tongue was almost her undoing.

And then it became a contest to see who could lick and suck better. Who could give the greatest pleasure.

She came first, screaming her bliss around the shaft in her mouth. Possibly smothering him as her body went boneless.

All of her quivered, especially her channel, and so when he released her, she flipped around on him until she straddled him properly. She splayed her hands on his chest and lifted her hips enough that her damp sex hovered above him. She even teased, letting the plump tip rub against her lower lips.

As if he had the patience for any more

teasing—she could tell he did not. His hands clasped her hips, and he thrust up as he held her steady, seating himself within.

She threw her head back and groaned. How could she not when the pleasure proved so intense?

She pushed down on him, impaling herself completely and feeling her still-quivering channel squeezing him all around.

The hands on her hips helped her to rock, driving him deeper, the pleasure of it an intense jolt, over and over, pressing against her sweet spot, making her breath catch.

And still he pushed into her, rocked her, gyrated on her so that all kinds of intensity tightened her body for a second orgasm. This time, he came with her, and through their bond, she felt his pleasure as if it were her own, and it amplified hers, making the waves roll one way then back. Over and over.

It was only as she huffed atop him, trying to catch her breath, that she groaned. "Dammit. We forgot to use a condom again."

"*I know.*" He smiled.

Epilogue

Despite all their searching, no one ever discovered the identity of the cloaked figure on the roof. After a while, interest in her waned given that the attacks had stopped. Whoever those humans worked for, whatever crazy group they belonged to, kept quiet and fell back into obscurity.

Despite beefed-up security at the Silver compound, no one so much as peeked in their direction. Much to their chagrin.

Of Samael, not a single trace was found. No one currently knew his whereabouts or his plans. Remiel wanted to hunt him but was stopped.

The advisor to the king, the very wise Silver, Waida, held Remiel back. "A king has more important things to worry about than a truant brother," she said.

And yet, he couldn't help but worry even as life went on.

With Anastasia gone and the Crimsons weakened by a lack of leader, they no longer had an interest in the next king and queen.

The ceremony to crown the Golden king went off without a hitch and was attended by everyone of importance from presidents to heads of Septs. Even some of the lesser races were invited, including shifters.

Sue-Ellen wisely had the dog treats and balls for fetching hidden before the shifter contingents' arrival. More than a few dragon faces scowled that she'd ruined their fun.

The massive feast was catered by some lion's pride looking to curry favor. Thick steaks, plentiful sides, and the most decadent desserts were offered, along with the most expensive of wines.

A good time was had by all, especially Remiel, who spent two weeks honeymooning with his angel on some isle.

For a while, things were good. The humans were fascinated by the royal pair. A tenuous peace existed around the world between humans, cryptozoids, and dragons.

The future seemed bright.

About eight months after the rooftop showdown—eight months of taking Sue-Ellen on a whirlwind tour of the planet—his angel gave birth to twins, a girl and a boy with crowning tufts of blond hair.

The pregnancy wasn't exactly planned; however, that first time they were together proved fruitful. So very fruitful.

But, thankfully, Sue-Ellen didn't mind. Since bonding with her new beast, she'd changed her view on certain things. For example, she now claimed the world revolved around her, not him.

She was right, and he gladly worshipped his queen.

Despite her initial trepidation, Sue-Ellen embraced the birth of their children and took to motherhood with enthusiasm. Now, if only Remiel could figure out how she did it so effortlessly. He struggled to be a good father. Especially during moments like now.

Remiel uttered a royal commandment. "Stop crying. I command thee."

The two most perfect angels, with eyes of pure gold, stared back at him, and continued to wail. And wail loudly. They possessed mighty sets of lungs. So mighty that his ears hurt.

Remiel shot a panicked thought at his wife.

"They aren't obeying!"

"That shouldn't surprise you given they're your progeny," Sue-Ellen said, not even trying to hide her mirth as she stepped into the room. "They need their diapers changed, which means you need to grab some wet wipes and a clean pair of diapers."

"Don't we have nannies for that?" He waved his hand in the direction of the miasma permeating from his ever-so-perfect children.

"It's their night off. So guess what, Daddy, you get to pitch in."

"A king doesn't wipe poop."

"A king will wipe poop if he ever wants sex again," she sassed nicely. "And don't forget the powder."

It was utterly undignified the things he did for his wife.

My queen.

But worth it. The riches he'd accumulated since his escape paled in comparison to the woman who had accepted him as mate.

Every day, she reminded him why life was

worth living to the fullest, and now she'd given him two extra reasons.

Two golden-haired dynamos with so much untapped potential. Many called him the dragon foretold, but looking at his progeny, Remiel had to wonder. The peace brokered with the other cryptozoids of note was tenuous at best. It wouldn't take much to topple. Anarchy lurked, waiting to pounce.

I can't wait.

The dragons had returned to the world, and it was their turn to rule.

*

The world wasn't burning.

Yet.

But the day crept ever closer.

It amused to watch the pretenders thinking they owned the throne. Ruling over their territory as if they had rights. Silly little ants really in the grand scheme of things.

The darkness of the cloak flowed as steps moved the body toward a hump in the corner.

Gold scales, dull and matted with filth and despair, rustled in agitation. A hand reached out to touch the prize. The captive dragon flinched, the head rearing back and causing the collar around a neck to ripple the fine chain holding it down. Holding the beast prisoner.

From almost leader to pathetic ruin.

My secret weapon. But a weapon that couldn't be revealed too soon. Things still had to move into position. But when the time came, nothing would stop the coming war.

The world would suffer wrath and vengeance.

And burn.

*Not quite the end. It seems poor Samael has been captured. But will anyone care enough to save him? STAY TUNED FOR **DRAGON REBORN**.*

CPSIA information can be obtained
at www.ICGtesting.com
Printed in the USA
LVOW07s1215140817
544943LV00002B/391/P

9 781988 328560